WHAT IF COMPASSION WAS NOT AN EMOTION THAT
EVOKED A RESPONSE,
BUT WAS A PRIZE TO BE WON?

THE

COMPASSION

PRIZE

KATY HOLLWAY

The Compassion Prize
Copyright © 2015 Katy Hollway

SozoPrint
SozoPrint.com

ISBN 978-0-9929404-3-0

Other titles from this author:

The Times of Kerim
The Days of Eliora

For Rachel,
I love the way you listen and then speak from your heart. You are
a true and inspiring friend

For PK,
Thank you for your amazing encouragement, friendship and
provoking words

... And for those that have stepped out
and shown true compassion

Chapter 1

He woke with a gasp. It was only a dream, not real at all. He rubbed his hands over his face to wipe away the sweat. He was safe, well, as safe as an Outsider could be. As his heart beat drumming in his ears slowed its pace he remembered why he was so anxious, and why dreams had plagued him for the past three nights. This was the first time he could get post.

He had heard it rumoured that life hadn't always been like this. The facts, however, were difficult to find when your resources were limited. He kept his ears open though, unlike most Outsiders who just continued as if this was their lot, as if this was all that mattered, as if their life no longer counted for anything.

He would have asked his grandparents the truth but he had never known them. The life expectancy for an Outsider was forty five years, although he did know of one shrewd old lady who reached fifty six. He had asked her once about it. She recommended keeping your wits about you and advised him to keep his head down. As if that were an existence. Within three months she was dead. Her wits had obviously run out on her.

Today was a day the Outsiders both dreaded and excitedly anticipated. Two times a year the post arrived. Two times a year twenty are selected. Two times a year two got the chance for Compassion.

The Compassion Prize could change everything. For those that won, their families enjoyed the comfort and security of Tropolis. The contestants never returned; win or lose, they were never seen again.

He thought about leaving this place and even the uncertainty could not cloud his hope. No one returned, that could only mean they were free from this place one way or another.

As soon as an Outsider reached fourteen, their name was highlighted on the Tropolis database and if they hadn't been selected by the time they were seventeen they remained an Outsider, to live out the rest of their life as one.

He had turned fourteen two months ago. That was why the arrival of the post brought mixed feelings. The anticipation made his stomach lurch.

His birthday had been marked only with the test that was taken each year; a thick stack of paper with numerous pictorial questions and multi-choice answers. No reading was required; it was just as well since most Outsiders had never learnt. He was an exception to the rule. This was the one thing his father had continued to teach him as a promise to his mother before she went.

The dream was already becoming a little hazy. A narrow bridge had stretched out over the deep-sided gorge. He knew he had to cross but the sight made him dizzy. Approaching, he had stepped gingerly onto the wooden boards. They gave a little under his weight. His heart quickened as a deep growling had come from behind. He had turned and briefly saw the red eyes peering at him through the jungle undergrowth. There had been no choice, he had to cross over. The bridge swayed with every hurried step. Fear overwhelmed him as he rushed towards the centre. Under his foot the board shuddered and snapped in two. He had felt himself falling ...

But it had only been a dream.

As the last residues of panic faded away the familiar tension began to rise.

He assumed that everyone felt the same the first time that they could be selected, but had very little to go on to confirm this.

With friendships ever at threat, Outsiders didn't make friends, at least not often and he was no exception. He had no friends and he would not tell them how terrified he was if he did. He hid it, tried to act normal with his dad, a man who didn't ask and who he was not sure that even cared. Outsiders never asked or offered that kind of information. To talk about how you felt showed weakness and an inability to cope with what life had dealt. He knew that feelings and emotions were a waste of already drained energy. There was little use in complaining anyway, no one could do anything to make it better.

He lay still for a moment, listening for movement. He heard the slow deep breathing from the other side of the room. His gasp hadn't woken his father. But it was no use, he knew he wouldn't sleep again, so he got up. He slung the empty rucksack over his shoulder before he pushed the door ajar. He peered back to check on his father who looked almost grey in the early morning light. He sighed, aware that he would never be able to blend in like that. His dark red hair made him almost one of a kind in this community. His mother, who he had inherited his russet hair and green eyes from, had celebrated it, but he hated being noticed.

He squeezed through the gap.

It was cold this early in the morning. The sun hadn't come up yet. Not that he complained. He preferred a chilly day. The stench was more bearable that way.

This time in the morning the city almost looked habitable. The darkness was great at hiding the lopsided shacks made of mismatched materials.

Many of the houses down this way were basic to say the least. There were places, however, made of preformed concrete and shipping containers closer to the walls of Tropolis. They were for the important members of the community, although he was not sure quite how they got chosen, since they didn't seem to do much for the Outsiders as a whole.

Tropolis, the place of the future. He saw it daily on the screens but as an Outsider he had never seen it with his own eyes. It was a place where he longed to be, a place of ease and comfort. The people there lived somewhere way beyond the wall and the Compassion gate. He thought he knew some of what went on. He had gleaned a little information from old newspapers, but even they were a rare find these days. He was not sure how they passed on their news anymore, but very little made it past the wall.

The passages were empty. There really was no need to get up until the barges delivered their loads, but he couldn't go back to bed. He was hopeful that maybe he would make a find while his world slept.

He quietly made his way through the maze of shanty houses towards the dump. The smell intensified as he got closer. He was grateful that his house was far enough away that on a good day, when the breeze blew in the right direction, the smell was whipped away. Today, there was no breeze and the stench hung in the air.

The chain-link fence that barely separated the homes from the dump had an unmanned gate, but in order to enter you had to be scanned. He lifted his wrist and put it up against the black panel. The gate clicked open, he stepped inside, the gate rattled as it shut behind him.

The hard packed roads were wider within the dumps to allow for the trucks that moved the waste to the incinerators where energy was produced, but at that time in the morning they were deserted highways haunted only by the waiting gulls. There would be nothing worth gleaning this far away from the heap but he didn't feel like a long walk. He wandered aimlessly up to the nearest pile yet to be moved to the vast power station, not really paying any attention to where he was going.

By far the best way to find anything of worth was to sort as you go. Gather the plastics in one bag, paper in another. Mixed gleans needed to be stripped before it was of any worth. If you were lucky you might find metal in cables or old technology. Traded metal would earn enough credits to buy things of the greatest value, like food to eat. Of course, there was food to be found at the dump too, but the food that could be bought at the Compassion gate hadn't been thrown away and tasted much better. He rarely had enough credits for that type of food as it was only him that gleaned for his family's survival.

When he was eight he had gleaned an old book, 'Growing Vegetables by Season'. He had almost lost it to another Outsider who knew that much paper would earn a credit, but thankfully he was quicker on his feet. But he had other plans for the valuable glean.

He consumed the details and learnt all that he could. He understood why the Tropolis resident had thrown it away, it was old fashioned compared to the glossy magazine he occasionally came across, but worth so much more than the credit had he traded it in. He gleaned containers that would hold soil and had success in growing some food. The seeds discarded by others in rotten food past eating still grew and when he did have to buy food, he chose wisely and saved whatever seeds there had been. Tomatoes were his favourite and very easy to grow, except in winter. He had a little success with strawberries in the hotter summer months. He had tried other plants too, such as pumpkin and corn. He stored whatever he could to carry himself and his father through, but winter months left them hungry and reliant on credits. He had to save his credits up to get them through those months.

He lazily pushed the top layer of rubbish over with his foot, not even attempting to bend low to investigate. Years of foraging had taught him to save his back from strain. He pressed his lips together in a tight line before weakly smiling to himself. Nothing, just as he had thought. This was all worthless and only good for potential power in the incinerator.

A little distance away, something glinted in the early morning rays. He kept focused on the spot as he picked his way across the heap.

A small ring pull from a drink can protruded out of the pile. Excellent. Not worth much on its own but that was not the point, each item brought a little more hope. He bent down to pick it out and was greeted by an even better find. The ring pull sat wedged within the pages of a thin pocket notebook. A double gleam.

The pages were fragile from the wet conditions, so he placed it carefully in his rucksack. He had tried to open a wet book before and only torn the paper, ruining it for anything other than trading. He had learnt to be patient and would let it dry out. He had the time.

He spent the rest of the morning in fruitless labour but was grateful that the time passed quickly. It wasn't long before other Outsiders were making their way to the far end where the barges docked laden with fresh rubbish. He dragged his feet, he didn't want to join them but knew that his father and himself needed to eat.

There was normally very little talk, but today there was even less. The post would arrive and they could all feel it, the potential for gain and also for loss.

Near the dock side stood razor wire fences taller than two fully grown men. The Tropolis workers said that the fences were to protect Outsiders from danger, from getting too near to the barges. The report had been that a couple of Outsiders had fallen into the water and been crushed in an accident several years ago when they had gotten too close to the unloading barges. There had certainly been deaths that day. The truth was less attractive. Several Outsiders had been shot, others had been drowned and even more injured as the force of Tropolis had exerted its control over the people. There was no medical assistance for Outside. He had keenly felt the loss every day since. He knew it would do him no good to linger over the sharp reminder.

There had been plenty more accidents on the unstable heaps since then, but after the refuse had been delivered it was no longer Tropolite responsibility as to how dangerous it was. Nothing was ever done to make them safe there.

It was Tuesday, so the Outsiders would be working the purple zone and the orange zone was out of bounds as the rubbish was moved and spread before being carried away to the incinerator. It normally took about two weeks for the sorted rubbish to be collected and burned. The less able Outsiders tended to frequent the spread refuse as the working zones could erupt into violence. Either way, before you gleaned you had to be scanned in.

All his hopes and fears seemed to be carried in his wrist and in the device implanted there.

A large concrete gateway separated the Outsiders from the heaps. The ever flickering sign above it indicated that the incinerator output was within the limits as it was lit by green numbers and the trade of reusable waste, the gleanings, were high. Both indicated that the Outsiders were desperate as much as Tropolis were extravagant and careless.

The queue was orderly. One at a time the Outsiders stepped up to one of the three archways, put their arm into the hole and had their chip scanned. They were recorded in and out of this place, 'for their own safety' of course. He scanned the chip at the turnstile all the while thinking that maybe he should have stayed away today.

A red light flashed above him and a horn sounded. The turnstile would not move. He was trapped between the barriers.

His heart began to race in a way reminiscent of the dream that had plagued him.

A Tropolis worker, in his neat green overalls strolled over to the archway, slid his pass key through the slot and smiled excitedly.

'This way number 57124. Follow me.'

He knew that everyone watched, because he would too. He hunched his shoulders as he approached the open ground and looked for a place to hide. Everyone must know that this wasn't just a little problem with his chip.

The Tropolis worker took him over to the small prefabricated office situated to the side where it monitored all the turnstiles. A tall man in a pale crisp suit, a very white shirt was pre-occupied with his silver communicator. He looked up, his eyes a little wide as if startled by seeing someone there. But quickly his face became stern as he held out a crimson package.

'Congratulations 57124,' the man said without a hint of enthusiasm. 'You have been selected to enter the competition for the Compassion Prize.'

Chapter 2

This was it. His whole future was sealed in the red envelope being handed to him.

It was strange. For a moment he wished he had never gone. He wished he had stayed away. But he knew they would have found him wherever he was. They had a way of knowing. How was that?

The flame red envelope felt like it was burning his hand.

An invitation to the competition, yet not an invitation at all if you wanted to be free from this place. It was a requirement to get out, the key to freedom and it was in his hand. Yet, he was still not sure if he wanted it or not. Freedom he wanted, but at what cost?

Suddenly the need to glean became urgent. If he was gone, how would his father survive? But with every eye seemingly focused on him in that moment, the only place he wanted to be is hidden away at home.

'Thank you,' he said with a dry mouth to the crisp- suited man, yet there was no change in the Tropolite's countenance; his expression remained one of disgust.

He stepped away nervously, certain that there was little else to say but not knowing if he had been dismissed.

The alarm sounded again and the light flashed above the far archway.

He watched as the green clad gate keeper scanned the card and opened the turnstile. A girl, maybe his age but a little shorter, was released. She followed the worker to the suited man who handed her a red envelope.

'Congratulations 43316, you have been selected to enter the competition for the Compassion Prize.'

He wondered if he looked that confident as he approached. He shook his head, certain that he hadn't. She stood straight and looked at the crisp man full in the face. The contrast was stark. His over clean, elegantly cut apparel to her brown and encrusted oversized coat with sleeves turned up and hem cut roughly. But it was their faces that captured the attention. The Tropolite looked down at her, with much the same expression, Outsiders were lower than him, too low, but she, well she was different, her face was not fearful or desperate, or full of expectation like others that had gone to the competition before. She was confident, almost as if she expected today to be her day, as if she knew she would be here, receiving the post.

There was no way to get away. He felt intimidated already. The turnstiles were still busy and the queue of gleaners stretched beyond the turnstiles. He anticipated an agonizing wait.

Only a moment passed before he realised that he was not standing alone.

'Are you going to glean?' she asked.

There she was. Her long trench coat skimmed the ground, her red envelope clutched in her hand.

He knew he should answer. 'I'm going home.' For the first time he looked in her face. She had wide grey eyes, a small button nose dotted with freckles and a narrow chin. Her face was framed by thick black hair. She reminded him of a porcelain doll he once saw. She had an open face, not like his. Anyone could see who she really was just by looking at her. She reminded him of his mother. He did not want to go there – not there, not then, not ever.

'Oh well,' she smiled a little sadly, 'I thought that maybe we could work together today.'

Together? Only semi functioning families worked together. 'No thanks. I need to head home.'

'Okay. I hope your father takes the news well.'

What? What did she know about him? He turned and faced her. 'Excuse me! How do you know about my father?'

'I'm sorry. Am I not supposed to know?' she whispered. 'I didn't mean anything by it. I know he isn't well and I just hope that the news gives him a little joy, that's all.'

Outsiders stared as they trundled past.

'It doesn't matter.' He waved his hand in dismissal. 'See you at the gate.' He hurried away and pushed through the tide of disgruntled Outsiders and out the arch. He had to get away.

The loud gulls called to one another as the barges arrived at the docks. Life happened behind him as he headed home, but was there life ahead of him too?

Reaching into his pocket he pulled out the red envelope. It was thick and heavy. He had never handled such a pristine object before. He frowned at the opportune yet hideous post. Shaking his head, he thought of the waste of paper, still, he could always trade it for credit.

His number was embossed on the rich surface and the flap was stuck down with some medieval looking wax seal. He broke the Tropolis T in half as he opened his post.

The card inside was the purest of white with artistically torn edges and fancy red swirls and swishes round the border. The Tropolite crest was printed in gold. There were very few words, but the ones that were there sent a shiver down his spine.

'Congratulations 57124, you have been selected to enter the competition for the Compassion Prize. Tomorrow, Compassion

Gate, 09:00.' The time and location were printed boldly underneath. There really was no need for instructions, everyone knew what the red envelope meant even if you couldn't read. But below, in small print was a short warning. 'Consider wisely if you wish to enter the competition as there will be no option to return to Outside or be re-entered.' It may have been short, but even that many words would have been a task for an Outsider to read. He thought, without arrogance and slight nervousness that he may be the only Outsider to receive post who could read the warning.

No option to return? What did that mean? The only way not to return was to be kept prisoner wasn't it? Or was there another way to prevent return? He had never seen anyone come home again. He had assumed that they had either won the prize, their family collected and lived a wonderful life at Tropolis, or that they had been given a lesser compassion and been allowed to stay alone, perhaps given work, menial work but better than here. He had an awful feeling that perhaps he had been naïve all this time.

With the threat still buzzing in his head, he shoved the card back into his pocket and entered the maze of streets. The common use of tarpaulin and collected planks or bricks formed the main structure of most homes.

There was no litter on the pathways but there was still a smell of decay. Everything was useful or had a use. In the doorways to their shacks small children played with some Tropolis child's rubbish.

He had to get out. There must be more to living than being someone's cast off. Everything had use or is useful, well perhaps this was his time to be useful, perhaps he could get them free.

He had to travel deep into the maze and out the other side before the branch of shanty houses and shacks that were his neighbours came into view. Near to the edge, tucked into the rock face the fused plastic casings of multiple discarded goods that formed the façade of his home came into view. It had been his idea to move this far out, away from the docks, away from the lavish containers. They had needed a quieter, less hostile place to exist, although, these days there were few reports of violence, people were just too tired trying to survive to think about death.

He slid the door to one side, ignored his father and filled a mug of rain water from the container in the corner.

It was cool.

He could feel his father's gaze but refused to turn just yet. He refilled the mug and then filled a second mug.

'Want a drink?' he asked as he put down the mug in front of his father.

The room was dark and his eyes were slowly adjusting.

He could see the frown and the question forming, but didn't really want to answer.

'Not much today,' he added. 'New book though. Needs drying.' He carefully lifted the notebook from the bottom of his bag and laid it in a patch of sunlight. 'Won't take long. Just a bit damp on the edges.'

His father watched him. 'Post day,' he mumbled.

The boy sighed. He thought his father had forgotten like so many other things. 'Yes. It is Post day.' He pulled the red envelope from his pocket and put it down next to his mug.

His father's head lowered and he let out a small gasp.

'I got the Post today,' the boy stated with as little emotion as possible.

'Too young,' he uttered.

'No. I'm fourteen.'

'Young.'

'Fourteen year olds have been selected before. There was another one just after me, a girl actually.' He started to feel anger rising up. 'I'm smart, I can do it.'

His father nodded because he knew that his son was capable. He took the mug in his shaking hand and tried to steady it before taking a sip. The man looked frail. His hair had fallen out in patches and he was dangerously skinny. 'Why you?' he finally asked. If anyone else had used such a small voice you would imagine them talking to themselves, but speech was difficult for this boy's father. He wanted an answer.

'It's random. They pick out twenty at random. The odds are going down, there just aren't as many of us as there used to be.'

'Not random.'

'What do you mean, not random?'

'Selection.'

'I don't know what makes me so special! But it doesn't matter. I could get us out of here.'

'Nothing to gain if you win.'

'Of course there is! We would get to be in Tropolis. Don't you want to be free?'

'Not freedom there,' his father said weakly. 'Not what you think.'

'Well it isn't freedom here.' He snatched up the notebook and turned to leave.

'Where's Willow?'

He turned back. His father's gaze was fixed on the damp notebook, but there was a faraway sound in his voice. His stomach tightened as he gritted his teeth.

'Mother isn't here anymore. She's gone.'

'That's right,' he sighed.

In that moment he knew he had to enter the Compassion Prize. He couldn't do this by himself in this rotting place anymore.

'I'm sorry Dad. I have to enter the contest. It is the only hope that we have.'

'Only hope in the death room.'

'What?' He was so hard to understand sometimes. The faraway look even suggested that he was not in the room anymore. This place was killing his father and if he didn't do something about it soon it would kill him too.

'Death.'

'I'm not going to die. I will win. I need to.' His father's face softened and his eyes closed. There would be no more words from him for a while and the boy didn't want to talk any longer. He went over to his bed, lifted the hatch in the wall at the end and climbed out. Tomorrow would come all too soon and he needed to make preparations.

The competition should be completed within the month, at least that was about the time the winner's family were taken to Tropolis. He didn't know that his father would be able to look after himself for that long.

There was little left of the vegetables to harvest. He picked the last marrow and inspected the pumpkin. It wasn't quite ready but it would have to do. He thought that his father could live off pumpkin soup for a while and whatever else the credits would buy. He had doubts that he could leave him, but he knew that he would. It was for his father's sake that he needed to do this. A niggling thought that rang loud: who was he trying to kid? He wanted to get out of this place, his father was just his excuse to go for the only escape route.

There was enough sun streaming through the clear corrugated plastic roof to the sheltered garden to dry out the pages of his find for today. He laid the notebook down, gently fanning it out to let the air circulate. The grey cover, though battered, still clung steadfastly to the wire spine. He could tell it had been used by someone, by the inked flower drawn on the front. It wasn't a flower he recognised. He curbed his curiosity knowing it would do no good to finger the pages. He would give it an hour or two and then investigate.

Back inside, he tipped the carton holding the thick plastic credits out over the bed. There weren't as many red as he would have liked to have seen, but plenty of brown. A quick calculation told him that there were 172 credits that could be redeemed; a balance that was being saved for the winter months. If he could budget it right, and get his father to agree, they could last until spring. The competition would be over, maybe within a month, so the credits would last longer than that if needed. With that grim, lingering thought, the boy knew that even with them his father would still starve, but it would take longer. There was no choice, he had to win or know his father would die.

Things would be different if his father would only glean but he had never seen him do it. With a desperate hunger, perhaps his father would get up and do something for himself rather than living off his son's hard efforts. Never had he gone to the gates, never had he provided for his family, never had he been a father. The boy was essentially alone and living with a parasite. He paused and hung his head, wondering if other Outsiders had such putrid revulsion in their minds.

He shook his head and sighed.

Being an Outsider had made him like this. He reached for the envelope and ran his finger over the broken seal. He dreamed of Tropolis, to be without an empty stomach, to live in comfort and happiness. There really was no choice, he had to win to be free.

Chapter Three

He woke very early. The same dream still lingered as he rubbed his hands over his face and eyes.

The thought came rushing. Competition day today.

'Blast! I forgot the notebook.'

He reached over to the hatch and clambered out. The sun had not risen fully or broken through the clouds that threatened rain. The book was still there although the pages were a little damp from resting on the moist ground. He still couldn't see if it was worth keeping or worth trading.

He went back inside, shivering slightly from the damp morning air, and draped the blanket over his shoulders. There was no chance of sleep so he laid the notebook on his bed.

He had so little time left in this shack that he would risk the emotions. Carefully he took the most precious of his books down from his cubby hole. It wasn't a book that had helped him to survive, as it didn't contain knowledge that would change the way he lived. It was just a simple children's story. His mother used to read it to him. He gently stroked the cover, remembering times when they used to pour over the illustrations, picking out the details and repeating the story over and over again. With it she taught him the extraordinary gift of how to read. For a year and a half she would read chapter after chapter to him, re-reading the book countless times. The cover was battered with wear and the pages yellowed. It was probably not worth more than a half credit, but priceless to him.

He missed her most when there was something he needed to talk about.

She would always be ready to listen. She didn't always have the answer but was able to take the burden.

He wished she was here to take it now.

Even if she were, he was not sure if he could put into words how he was feeling. But she would know.

He missed her.

She would often congratulate him on his 'Good Choice!' He felt right now, that he had no choice left. That option had been taken away from him.

He needed to take his mind off her. He needed a distraction.

It was still a little too delicate, but he could be careful and that would help take his mind from his mother.

The flower on the cover was so unusual and had been hand drawn. Five petals, like elongated hearts had a hint of pink in them. In the centre, it looked to have a split stigma, surrounded by a twist of filaments. It reminded him of the faded green botanical book his mother used to have. The illustration style was very similar. Not helpful. He needed distracting.

He almost ripped the cover off in his haste to get away from studying it.

Page after page were full of numbers and letters in columns. Some were crossed out while others were underlined. They meant nothing.

The drink can ring was still caught in the damp pages. He gingerly peeled them apart. This page was different. In neat handwriting was written:

Compassion - testing
Death room = danger
*Rubbish hatch

Today, of all days to see that word again. Compassion. He knew that the Compassion prize was awarded to the one who wins the competition so testing makes sense. But to see death room written down. Didn't his father mention that yesterday? He didn't understand so he eased apart the next pages looking for answers.

There followed half a dozen pages with various two letter combinations next to six digits and then four. The system and pattern seemed familiar but he couldn't put his finger on it. The same number sequence assigned for several letters then it changed, but only slightly.

He adjusted the blanket to sit more snuggly around his shoulders.

The last few letter number chains were incomplete. Then that was it. Nothing else. Over half the little book empty.

He turned back to the notes. The word compassion glared at him.

He sat, staring at that page for quite some time, fears, hopes and unknowns rushing through his head. On a whim, he decided to add it to the bag with the few possessions that would be going into Tropolis with him.

He picked up the credits that were bunched together with elastic bands and called to his father to wake up. He grunted.

'I've got to go. Wake up. You need to listen for a moment.'

His father turned over and looked up sadly. He remembered what day this was.

'When they come to collect you, I want you to bring all my things, do you hear me?' His father nodded. 'I've split these up into weeks,' the boy said as he showed him the bundles of credits. 'You've got to be careful not to overspend.' His father nodded again. 'I mean it.'

'Yes. Keep safe.'

'Don't worry about me.'

'Love you, Luca.'

Luca turned and left, frowning at such an outburst.

He didn't want to think about loss. He bit down on his lip as he remembered his bitterness that had surfaced the day before.

Saying goodbye made it too final. Instead he found comfort in his use of his name.

Names were never used. No one officially had one. His mother used to call him Luca and she would not respond to his father unless he called her Willow. She would say, that just because they lived as Outsiders, doesn't mean they cannot be given the dignity of a name as it costs nothing. But it did cost. Soon after his mother was gone, there was a shut down on the use of any names, even nicknames. If a Tropolite worker heard the use of a name, there was trouble. There were stories of severe beatings circulated after insider information had been given, but Luca had never seen any evidence. The habit of using registration numbers then became natural and friendships died out. Names were reserved only for the Tropolites.

Luca's bag was hardly stuffed full, but weighed heavily on his shoulders.

The streets were full of Outsiders heading for the docks. Luca joined the silent throng as they threaded through the narrow passages.

He could hear voices up ahead and strained to see what the noise was about. The group were nearing the gate. Luca's last journey with fellow outsiders is almost done.

People were calling out and a solitary voice female answered each time.

'Thank you ... I'll do my best ... Take care of yourself ... Look after each other ... I'll miss you!'

There she stood. Number 43316 in her oversized trench coat. She answered the calls of Outsiders as they wished her well. How did they all know her? The Compassion contestants never got a send-off like this. Luca saw a younger Outsider run to her and get lost in the folds of the coat. 43316 bent down, whispered in the little one's ear then kissed them on their cheek. The mother stood a short distance away and blew a kiss as her child dashed back to her.

Luca shuffled to one side feeling uncomfortable. His people did not act this way.

As the Outsiders left her, they chatted to one another. The silence was broken. One smiled at another.

Luca held back to listen to the conversation.

'You know her too?'

'Oh yes! The sweetest girl.'

'I shall miss her.'

'How do you know her?'

'You know what, I don't recall! But she is always so ...'

'... generous!'

'Like no one I've met.'

'Mind you, who have we ever really met?'

'That is true.' They laughed together.

'You gleaning green today? Do mind if I join you?'

'Yes, why not!'

Outsiders were choosing to talk, choosing to be friends? Luca rubbed his eyes once again thinking that he must be imagining it all, but he glanced round to see another couple shaking hands, a group of three were laughing together and even more were indulging in chatter.

He backed away from them.

He didn't understand.

He found himself in the only place where there were no Outsiders, near to the Compassion Gate and next to the strange girl.

She continued to call out, waving and smiling at so many of the Outsiders as they filed past on their way to the port.

It wasn't long before they were joined by eight others. All were taller, older and more menacing than Luca. Suddenly, this little girl seemed like the only one that Luca could beat in this competition. Even more come wandering over and soon there was a silent crowd.

Luca had a brief moment of doubt. He thought he should run while he had the chance.

The sound of booted footsteps alerted Luca to a new arrival behind him.

Luca spun round and came face to face with the same Tropolite man that handed him his invite. His crisp clothes and white shirt were un-crumpled and his stern face remained unchanged as he scrutinised the group.

'Missing two already.' he stated with no emotion. 'Hold out your wrists.'

The others lined up. Luca shuffled to the end of the line, thinking of breaking free.

'I'm glad you're here. I was hoping you'd come.' She had a clear voice, even in her whispered tone.

'Are you talking to me?' Luca asked.

'Of course I'm talking to you! You said you were coming, so I decided I would too.'

Luca was debating whether he had what it took to escape and was just about to make a run for it when a dark skinned boy with a faded black baseball cap planted himself next Luca.

'You nearly missed it!' The girl said as she leaned around Luca.

'You said I should be here, so I am.' he answered back, pushing the cap up away from his bright eyes.

The suited man approached the girl, ran the scanner over her wrist and then held it up to take her picture. She stood as tall as she could and smiled.

Luca was so taken aback by her pose that he failed to move. He ran out of time to escape.

'Wrist,' the crisp Tropolite man commanded.

Luca held it out. He was scanned and photographed and was sure that his image was nowhere near as confident as hers.

'Ah! A late comer. You nearly missed your chance.' The stern face almost became a sneer.

'Not gonna happen,' the boy in the black cap said, adding a lopsided smile to the photographic collection as he hummed.

There they were, nineteen out of the twenty. The competitors for Compassion.

'Follow me,' the Tropolite commanded.

Chapter 4

Luca had never walked through the gates.

He had peered through so many times, hoping to see what was beyond his life but there was nothing to see. The concrete wall that was punctured by the gate was repeated further in, blocking any view. A double line of captivity, as if one was insufficient hold anyone on the Outside.

A series of tuneful beeps issued from the scanner as the Tropolite tapped in a code and the gates eased open. Luca felt a sudden coldness spread over him. A rusty screeching from the gates would have been a little more reassuring than the dead silence. It unnerved him and he gasped as he felt the pinch he made on his wrist.

The boy wearing the black cap tipped back the rim, looked up and hummed the series of notes from the code. His cheerful face, and lopsided smile did not betray any fear, if he was feeling it at all. Luca was certain he was the only one who felt uncomfortable.

The gates towered over them as they approached. The metal bars with gaps only wide enough for a hand to slip between hung from thick concrete walls. If they could be gleaned they would feed half of the Outsider community through the winter without fail yet they stood untouched and mocking.

The line of Outsiders filed through into the shadow of the wall on the other side.

The Tropolite, in his crisp white suit and crisp stern face, marched on. He paused only to ensure everyone had come through the gates before repeating the code once more. Luca copied the melody in his head. He followed after the girl he called Smiler. Her long coat, with its trimmed hem, brushed the ground leaving slight swirls in the dust. Her dark hair that reached halfway down her back, bounced as she walked. Black Cap walked closely behind him, humming some light-hearted tune. Luca turned and looked at him irritably.

They waited, dwarfed by the massive concrete wall hiding the other world beyond it. The wall ran featureless to the left and right as far as could be seen into the gloom.

'Follow me,' Crisp commanded taking the left passage and was quickly flanked by two other Tropolite workers or guards.

Luca didn't know where else he would go and nervously sought out the other option. A green clad Tropolite materialised from the gloom and blocked the way. Black Cap nudged him to follow the others.

The echo of their feet clattered and scratched along the passage killing any sound that may have drifted down from above. A tall boy, which walked directly behind Crisp, coughed and then sniffed. Crisp turned his head slightly and his eyes narrowed. Smiler hadn't said a word but she did just that, smiled, as she turned towards Luca. Luca looked on her suspiciously, not sure what she wanted from him. He frowned a little and shrugged his shoulders.

Luca's eyes had finally adjusted to the filtered light. The dull white walls glistened and the drainage channels at the base ran with water.

Crisp stopped at the first real feature that they had seen. He unbuttoned the cuff of his shirt and pulled back his sleeve before slipping his arm into the dark hole. A set of double doors that they had not noticed slid apart in the wall next to him. He quickly removed his hand and wiped it with the handkerchief from his pocket. He stepped briskly into the space about the size of an Outsiders room and turned towards the group. The guards ushered them forwards. They all followed. Then the guards stepped in and the doors closed. Luca hated being this close. His ears began to buzz and he felt sweat forming on his neck.

Suddenly his stomach lurched as the space began to sink.

Luca was not the only one to be surprised. Several competitors gasped and one or two of them reached out for something to hold onto. The tall boy coughed and sniffed repeatedly. Crisp and the guards exchanged glances. They seemed completely composed. Luca decided that imitating them is the best policy despite wanting to prise open the doors for air to breathe.

Eventually the sinking feeling slowed and stopped, causing his stomach to lurch again. The doors slid apart and a waft of warm salty air mixed with grease filled the small space. Luca filled his lungs and blew out slowly. He didn't want to throw up.

The white walled corridor was gone.

The guards stepped out, followed speedily by Crisp who took out a small canister from his jacket pocket and sprayed something into his mouth. The group of potential contestants filtered out behind the officials before the swish of the doors closed.

Long strip lights flickered on the low curved ceiling. They illuminated what looked like the dock edge, only, there was no wide sky or water lapping at the side and it was much shorter than an actual barge, ending abruptly with plain white walls. A wide concrete plinth, with a metal strip attached to it, ran parallel to the dock edge and as far as could be seen into the tunnel beyond. Luca thought that he could jump the gap between the edge and the plinth, but was hoping, and guessing that was not what they want them to do. He couldn't imagine

Crisp throwing himself out over the gap. There seemed no other way out.

A muffled female voice materialised.

'Stand clear!'

Crisp and the guards stepped forward confidently and without concern. Each one looked to the right hand tunnel.

A faint rumble was coming from the tunnel and a gust of air blew across Luca's face as he turned. A triangle of clear light was moving towards him. Luca stepped away, unnerved by the sudden movement towards him.

The vehicle slowed as it reached the dock edge then halted.

It was sleek and polished. The dull strip lights glimmered on the curved sides and top.

'Enjoy your journey on Tropolis Maglev Monorail!' the bodiless female added.

A panel of the side of the monorail train gently moved out towards him with a hushing sound then slid up and over the roof.

The guards ushered them onto the second compartment before they joined Crisp in the first.

Luca saw Crisp through the glass walls. He sat with his back to them in his luxurious train. Luca's space had hard plastic moulded benches. As Luca was one of the last to board there were no spaces to sit alone. Smiler smiled at him. Luca shrugged and thought that there would be no harm in sitting with her, just as long as he kept his distance. She shifted over, wrapping her coat around herself and over her lap to make space for him. Luca thought that the fabric would be able to go round her several times. Black Cap joined them. He briefly took off his cap and scratched his head casually. Nothing seemed to shake this boy's confidence.

'Welcome to Tropolis!' said one of the competitors sarcastically. He was a strangely thickset and muscular boy, not a common feature for the poverty stricken Outsiders. No one replied. They all knew their place. 'I'll sit there one day,' he stated, glaring into the back of Crisp's head.

The train moved almost silently. There was a little bit of vibration but that was all.

There was nothing to see out of the windows. Luca saw only his own reflection and thought about the mess that looked back at him.

Luca sat in silence and he began to wonder how far they needed to travel, what he would need to do to win the prize and if he would ever see his father again. He pulled the bag from his back and hugged it to himself. He focused on his fingers fiddling with the clips. The click, click, click of the clip fastening and unfastening steadied his heart a little.

A small hand touched his and he winced.

'It will be alright.' Smiler mouthed so that only Luca could understand her.

He pulled his hands away and puffed. He couldn't have them thinking he was weak if he was to win. He vowed in that moment never to show any weakness.

Thickset looked down his wide nose at Luca but Black Cap gestured back to him leaning forward, hands on knees as if he was ready for a fight. Thickset batted it away with a hand and turned back to eye Crisp.

Luca turned slightly and frowned towards Black Cap who nodded back protruding his lower lip in a wonky smile. Luca pulled away wondering why they thought he needed protecting.

There was something un-natural about the lack of chatter in the carriage. Outsiders have never been especially talkative to one another, but Luca thought that this would have been a good place to stand together, a united front. But then he remembered, they weren't united, they were to be set against each other. Nineteen and only a pair of them could or would win.

The periodic cough and sniff punctuated the silence.

It was difficult to tell how fast they were travelling through the dark tunnel but they sat for a long time before the train reduced its speed.

Warm light flooded the train as it stopped. The blank white walls were far behind them, here the curved walls and ceiling were embellished with mirrors and the plain functionality of the Outsider world had been replaced with elegance.

The door slid upwards and the other contestants stepped out. Luca hung back only to be pushed forward by Black Cap.

The mirrored vaulted ceiling threw hundreds of reflections back at Luca. Each face he saw seemed to tell him he was not alone. Some looked scared while others were excited, one or two seemed nervous but most of all, they were all out of place. Luca wanted to get back on the train and get away from this place. He didn't care that he would have to glean forever. He didn't think he could survive in this place. A trickle of sweat ran down the back of his neck and his breathing became shallow.

Crisp walked on, unconcerned, through a sweeping archway. Despite Luca's urge to flee to the open and waiting train, he followed all the others. Glancing up he saw the words lining the arch and struggled to believe them.

WELCOME TO TROPOLIS

Chapter 5

Luca was thankful that Crisp took them to the flight of polished concrete stairs and he didn't have to endure the stomach turning box again.

After fifty steps, Thickset was looking red in the face and the coughing boy was wheezing heavily, but the climb was not over. The stairs zigzagged higher.

'Please … can we wait … just … a short break?' Thickset called out.

Crisp ignored him and kept marching on.

Many of them used the handrail as they followed after him. None of the Outsiders were used to stairs.

After another fifty steps the air became cooler. Luca thought that they must be coming to the end. The next turn made his eyes sting and he squinted into the blast of bright sunlight streaming from above. Vast sheets of glass were held suspended above them with a simple steel framework. It reminded him of the illustrations of a greenhouse in his book with them being the seedlings emerging from the dirt.

He was lost in the beauty of the open space as his eyes adjusted. The white floor glistened. The slabs of highly polished stone with veins of grey and black, flowed through the space reflecting the steelwork and glass. The room was completely empty bar the stairwell and a series of frosted glass doors set into the wall opposite, not even flakes of dust danced in the sunlight.

Luca frowned. The day had been grey and cloudy where he lived. Maybe Tropolis was further away than he had thought.

Suddenly all the doors opened at exactly the same time.

'One person per room,' Crisp instructed. 'Go!' he added impatiently.

The only way was forward. Perhaps this was a test. Luca wanted to be sure that he had no reason to blame another for his choice so quickly strode to the door second from the end, paused momentarily and entered. He could hear the others choosing their doors before his closed softly behind him.

'Place your arm in the scanner,' the metallic female voice said.

Luca was in a small, square white room. White again. Was there no colour in Tropolis? All the surfaces looked as if they were made of one large piece of moulded plastic including the rounded light set into the ceiling, the seat, the deep arch and the scanner hole in the wall.

'Place your arm in the scanner,' she repeated with no sense of impatience.

Luca did as he was told.

'Welcome to Tropolis number ...' There was a pause as he was read and an emotionless voice recited his number. '57124. Remove all your clothing and stand in the zone marked.'

A square of light glowed from the floor in the archway opposite.

'All? Why?'

He waited but got no reply. He couldn't stay there forever. He reluctantly removed everything and stood on the square.

Beams of violet light from the archway ran over him.

'Scanning complete. Move forward and step into the shower.'

The back panel of the arch slid to one side.

Luca leaned over to his clothes and pulled the bag from underneath. He had a feeling that he wouldn't see his clothes again and as he walked through the arch the panel slid shut behind him.

No sooner was it shut than hot water sprayed at him from all directions. The waste water ran murky. Luca couldn't help but sigh as the water became foamy, soft and scented, he could feel it lifting the dirt from his skin and hair. The sequence repeated three times and he felt shrivelled when the water finally stopped. Warm air blew throughout the room, drying the droplets and moisture from every surface.

A different door slid open and the voice spoke one more time.

'Put on your new clothes and proceed to the waiting area.'

Luca almost forgot his bag. It was still soggy, obviously not as easy to dry as skin and plastic.

The third space was a mirror image of the first, but on the chair lay folded clothes that were not his own. Luca felt exposed again. Were they monitoring him even here, was this all a test? There was nothing else to do but slip on the trousers and shirt. They fitted really well and the material was warm against his skin. He had been right to retrieve his bag but knew that he couldn't walk out with it. It's battered and dark material would stand out against the pale creams and whites of his new clothes. He found pockets in his trousers but little way of concealing anything else.

He crouched down and opened the bag.

The small notebook sat on the top of the pile. He slipped it hurriedly into his pocket. He had a strong feeling that the others shouldn't know that he could read. He thrust his hand into the bag once again.

The swish of the doors made Luca jump. Suddenly, he was exposed to the other side of the vast open room.

'Leave that,' Crisp commanded. 'You are the last and we have been waiting for you.'

Thickset sneered at Luca from the plush chair he was lounging on. He was dressed, as were all the contestants, in white or cream.

Smiler looked smaller somehow, but cleaner. The old trench coat was gone and she stood in a flowing white dress, dainty jacket and white pumps. She looked younger than Luca now.

It was only when Luca got offered a hand to help get up from the floor that he realised Black Cap was there. His black cap was gone, but a mass of black curly hair reached his shoulders.

'Come on then. Time to move on,' he said.

Luca stared at the last fragment of himself, and winced as he would have to leave it behind. He wanted to scream and grab it anyway, but Thickset already considered him weak and he didn't want to add anything to that idea. He took a deep breath, refused Black Cap's help and got up.

Crisp led the group over to a desk at the far end where an elegant Tropolite woman was sat at a screen.

'Scan there,' she pointed to the glass gap at her desk. Luca was fascinated by her bright red nails.

Thickset moved forward and ran his wrist over the scanner.

'Station two.' She pointed down the corridor to her left. 'Next.'

Luca peered round to see where she had indicated.

There were large mirrors on the walls with a wide soft chair in front of each. Standing behind each chair were three Tropolites, immaculately dressed in the now familiar white but with royal blue accents.

Thickset strolled off, full of confidence.

One after the other, the competitors were sent to different chairs.

Luca was sent to station six where he was ushered into the luxurious seat.

All the competitors were seated. Luca glanced to the sides and checked in the reflection and there were two stations left empty. Twenty spaces, eighteen seats occupied, but weren't there nineteen in total?

Everyone looked so different in their clean clothes that it took Luca some time before he noted the absence of coughing and sniffing. Crisp seemed unruffled and no one else had said a word. Luca recalled how Crisp had said he was the last, but where was that boy?

'Now this won't hurt much. It will just be a scratch.' A woman dressed in white with a red belt, held Luca's hand, palm up and punched a needle on the tip of his finger. The shock made him flinch and forget about other competitors. The woman squeezed a drop of blood onto a card and then inserted it into the slot in the wall.

'What was that for?'

'Just running a few checks,' she said innocently smiling at him. 'Carry on,' she instructed the blue Tropolites behind.

'Now if you would just sit up straight we can sort out your hair.'

Luca did as he was told, but watched the red belted woman move to the Outsider in the next station and repeat the process.

The gentle tug on his hair drew Luca's attention back.

'How lovely to have you with us! My name is Franco and I am here to beautify you. You have lovely thick hair. What I am going to do is take out some of this length, shorter is the fashion at the moment. Then I'll add a bit more texture.'

Luca just nodded a little and watched what he was doing the reflection. It was incredibly strange to be this close to others and Luca was desperate to pull away from their touch.

Curls of russet hair tumbled to the floor as Franco snipped away. Franco, the first person to have a real name and use it. He chattered away, not only to Luca but also to his two assistants who were buffing Luca's nails and applying lotion to his face.

Luca couldn't remember the last time his hair was this short, tidy or clean. He looked different, less like an Outsider, less like himself.

'There you go young sir! You almost look the height of fashion now! I've left it a little longer on top and run some product through it to give you some extra texture. I think you could pass for a Tropolite now!' Franco implied Luca should be grateful for his transformation. 'You have quite good skin.' Then he lowered his voice to a whisper. 'Better than that kid over there. They have had to do some remedial work on that complexion! I have never seen such a bad case!' Luca turned to see who Franco was talking about. 'Don't look!' he admonished. 'You my dear should do very well indeed. I hope to see you tomorrow.'

Luca carefully examined his reflection. He could still see traces of the Outsider. His hair, although shorter still suited him, but made him look older, but maybe he was just older from the last time he really looked. He smiled a little and his green eyes crinkled. He didn't know what they put on his face but it felt really soft as he reached up to touch it. The faded dark circles under his eyes and his rounded nose made him look like his father, but overall, his face shape and hair colouring was more like his mother's.

Luca turned. 'Thank you Franco.'

'He has manners too! Bless!' Franco patted Luca's shoulder. 'I really do hope that I see you tomorrow.'

'I hope so too Franco. Any tips?'

'Now, now, it isn't up to me who gets chosen!' Then he lowered his voice once again, rested his arm on Luca's shoulder and bent low to Luca's ear. He was so close, Luca could see the lump from Franco's scanner in his wrist. Luca cringed inwardly at the contact. 'I would say that you should charm them, make them feel comfortable with you. But I didn't say anything, you hear me?' And he winked.

Charm them? How exactly and who would he need to charm?

His questions didn't have time to surface. The contestants were being ushered back to the waiting room.

41

Thickset looked menacing as he moved past with his incredibly short hair exposing his wide shoulders. He knew it too. He strutted over to the biggest sofa and deposited himself on it taking up as much space as possible.

Black Cap had his hair cut in a similar style to Luca, but with his dark skin and large eyes he looked angelic. Luca thought he would have no problems with charm.

Smiler almost floated over to Luca. Her hair had been left long, but all the tangles were gone and there were dark shiny ringlets arranged elegantly in their place. A simple ribbon pulled her hair away from her face. 'You look terrified,' she said smiling. 'Just try to relax.'

'You don't know anything,' Luca replied, frustrated that she could read him so well.

Crisp was organising them into a line and taking their picture yet again with his scanner. Luca remembered to smile a little, he wanted to charm whoever was going to look at him.

A bell rang from the desk.

'Go through now,' the red nailed woman instructed them.

Crisp lead the way to the large double doors behind her. They opened as he approached and he went in followed by the group of Outsiders dressed as Tropolites.

'Please, I want to be your friend,' Smiler said quietly.

'I don't have friends,' he mumbled distractedly.

'Well, maybe you should give it a go,' she added sadly, brushing the hair over her right shoulder.

Luca couldn't help but stare. On her neck was a small tattoo in the shape of a familiar flower. Luca instinctively reached into his pocket. The flower on his notebook.

.

Chapter 6

The amazing aroma set Luca's stomach rumbling.

Food, masses of it, was laid out on a long table. Huge plates with glossy roasted meat, bowls filled with coloured fruits, dish after dish with differing sauces and open baskets heaped with fresh bread. The colour saturated the air as much as the scent.

'Help yourself,' Crisp said, glaring a little before disappearing through a thick panelled door.

Luca was just about to dash forward when Smiler pulled on his sleeve. 'There is plenty to go round. Take it slowly, you are being watched.' She raised her chin. Luca looked up and see the blinking red light of a recording camera in the corner of the room. It seemed that Smiler was right.

The other contestants had hands full and crammed mouths and Luca was desperate to join them.

He walked slowly over to the table, taking time to enjoy the soft carpet beneath his feet and the unusual canvas paintings on the stark walls. He was doing his best at distracting himself from behaving like the others.

Black Cap offered him a small plate. Luca wished it were bigger, there was so much there that he wanted to taste, but he loaded it carefully with a little of the meat, bread and fresh fruit.

Smiler acknowledged how difficult this was with a little sigh and joined Luca away from the temptation of the food laden table.

'What would be wrong with that?' Luca asked between restrained bite-sized pieces of succulent meat and crunchy bread.

'Everything is a test. If we want to win over the Tropolites we need them to accept us.'

'Why are you helping me?'

'Because I want you to do well.'

Luca frowned at her.

'Friends?' she asked.

Black Cap was standing by the table having taken a large chunk of soft cheese. 'Mercy,' he said, 'he doesn't want friends.'

'Outsiders don't do friendship,' Luca agreed.

'This one does. I think we could give it a go.'

Luca turned away.

'See, I told you,' Black Cap ribbed.

'We need to give him a chance, Eban,' Mercy responded and turned again to Luca. 'I know that we look after ourselves normally, but here we need to look out for each other.'

'This is a competition. We should behave like competitors.' Luca reminded her.

'Who says? Would you have us act like enemies before we have even begun? Maybe as friends we have a better chance.'

'I saw you,' Luca said accusingly, 'you don't act like an Outsider. You had everyone talking back home before we came here.'

'I may not act like one, but I am more of an Outsider than anyone else here. Give it a go. My name is Mercy.'

'Outsiders don't have names.'

'I do, Eban does and so do you.'

'How do you know that?'

'Everyone has a name, but not everyone knows it. Well, you do don't you? What is it? We can't get into trouble here for having a name.'

'You sure?' Luca asked nervously.

'Look, you have heard them using names haven't you? Have we done anything to make you not trust us?'

Luca had to admit that they seemed genuine and shook his head. What real harm was there in letting them help him? He would be careful. 'Luca. My name is Luca.'

'Well Luca, it really is lovely to meet you,' Mercy said smiling broadly.

'Do you know what is coming next?' Luca asked.

Eban leaned forward and whispered. 'No one knows. But they haven't beautified us for no reason at all. Best stay clean and how they want us for now.'

There was some wisdom in that. Luca was certain Eban was right. He peered down and straightened his shirt.

'Have you tried the spiced rolls?' said Eban through a mouthful. 'There are amazing. Go on, take one.' Eban placed one on Luca's plate. Luca instinctively turned it over to check for mould before biting into it.

The other contestants were still attacking the food when Crisp re-entered.

'60158 this way,' he read from a silver hand held device.

Thickset looked torn between following Crisp and the delicious food. Luca couldn't help but snigger. It didn't go unnoticed. Thickset narrowed his eyes and balled his greasy fists.

'Now,' commanded Crisp.

They left through the panelled door.

Mercy shrugged as Luca looked at her questioningly.

The room was still for a few moments before the lure of food took over once again.

Nine more contestants were escorted through the door by Crisp but they didn't come back.

Luca lost his appetite.

'41125,' Crisp announced.

'That's me,' said Eban. 'Stay calm Luca, I'll see you and Mercy on the other side!' He strolled off with confidence humming a tune as he went.

'He's right. Just smile, be likable and friendly, I'm sure it will be fine,' Mercy said patting Luca's arm which he moved away. 'Try not to panic.'

'I'm not panicking.' Luca defended, although he could feel that line of sweat running down his neck again.

The door opened much more quickly than before.

'57124.' It was Luca's turn.

Mercy smiled as he walked past her. His feet felt heavy and his breathing seemed laboured.

Crisp held the door open while Luca went through.

A long white corridor stretched out before him, lit by high level windows. Luca looked up and saw the cyan blue of the sky through the topmost panes and a few punctuations from tall glass buildings. Small flashing red lights told Luca that he was being watched.

Crisp marched on ahead, his feet metallically tapping on the hard floor. There was nothing left but for Luca to follow.

There were a number of door alcoves along the corridor, but Crisp didn't stop until he reached the double doors at the far end. He paused. 'You shouldn't have entered the Prize,' he hissed. 'But since you are here, I suggest you make them like you.'

Crisp opened the double doors. Luca looked at him and frowned. Yet another Tropolite had given him advice. Crisp failed to make eye contact, let Luca pass, then shut the doors between them, leaving Luca stood by himself in a plain, white round room. In front of him there was a large Network screen showing two male and two female Tropolites.

Luca's appearance in the room registered within the screen beside the panel.

'Cleaner than most of the others,' said a disembodied voice. Luca looked down at his shirt and noticed a few crumbs.

'Good height,' another commented.

Luca stood up straighter, unsure of how they were able to assess him accurately.

'A fairly pleasant face.'

As the Tropolite panel spoke to one another their responses and comments appeared next to his picture.

He did his best to smile. He must charm them, despite his fear.

'Now that is better!' chirped the woman from the far right smiling back with pristine dark red lips. 'We need to add a name to your entry. Would you like to choose or shall we?'

He was allowed a name. Should he give the name his mother had given him? 'Good afternoon,' he began, 'Thank you very much for having me in Tropolis.' All but one of the panel seemed pleasantly surprised at Luca's manners. 'If it pleases the panel, I would choose Luca.'

'Luca it is.'

'Luca' appeared in blue letters on the screen above his head and 'polite' labelled him. He was being charming and they seemed to be lapping it up.

'Welcome to Tropolis Luca,' the red lipped lady again addressed Luca before proceeding to read off the silver communicator in her hand. 'Over the next period of time you will be tested and rated according to your performance in a number of tasks. According to your abilities you will be scored, with the contestant with the highest ranking gaining the much revered Compassion Prize. It is your duty to do your best at everything that is set before you.' It seemed odd that he needed to be told to do his best. Surely, in order to gain the prize that would be obvious. 'Before you ask,' she continued now looking up at Luca, 'We cannot divulge the nature of the tests.'

'I understand.'

'You will be given enough preparation time on certain tasks to be able to put your best effort forward.' Then she turned to her male colleague. 'Test results from the Deoxyribonucleic Acid and blood enzyme check?'

'Basically clear. There are a few anomalies but nothing we haven't seen before.'

'Well, in that case Luca, you are free to leave.' She pressed a button on her communicator. 'You will be shown to your room.'

One of the guards that had escorted the Outsiders to Tropolis opened a door to the left stood waiting.

'Thank you for your time. Good bye.' Luca turned and left the room.

The corridor beyond was featureless and low ceilinged with frosted glass walls. Shadows of people moving around on the other side made Luca feel enclosed. Luca was used to open skies and single room buildings. He had not breathed Tropolis air yet, he had not felt the breeze. The more he considered the maze of rooms he had already been taken through, the deeper the building seemed to suck him in. He took a deep breath and concentrated hard on the tapping feet of the guard in front. These people were secure and confident, but then he remembered, they were Tropolites and were not in this contest.

After taking numerous turns, Luca and the guard finally stopped before a grid work of steel and glass. The guard pushed on a button which began to glow white.

'What are we waiting for?'

'Elevator.'

Luca had no idea what he was talking about so stood patiently.

The space in front of them began to fill with the descending floor and glass walls of what Luca now understood as an elevator.

Luca couldn't swallow and his hands began to shake.

'Can't we take the stairs? There are stairs right?'

'I'm not climbing the stairs that far,' the guard said, smirking. 'Get in.'

Luca repeated to himself the promise to not appear weak and stepped in.

The doors began to slide smoothly together.

'Hold the lift!' called a man rushing towards them.

Luca's guard punched a button beside him and the doors reopened. Luca was astonished to see Eban standing there with another guard. He feared he'd seen the last of Eban. But Eban had survived the test so far.

'Thought you had already gone up,' Luca's guard commented.

'Needed the bathroom.' His colleague jerked his head towards Eban.

'Couldn't it wait?'

'Apparently not. They'll need me for the next one. Can you take it up?'

'Forbid it that you would get into trouble.' And Luca's guard nodded.

Eban stepped in leaving the other guard outside. The doors closed this time and sealed with a small hush. There were three buttons available. The guard had used one to hold the doors open. The other two were positioned above and below a grid. He pushed the top one.

The glass box rose exceptionally fast. Luca grabbed the cold steel bar tightly. They had travelled rapidly through two floors and Luca had caught glimpses of identical corridors to the one he left behind. He felt his stomach churn and closed his eyes hoping that this journey would not take too long. Bright light warmed his face and coloured his eyelids red. Cautiously, he peered out. Sunlight steamed into the elevator as it shot up the side of the building. They were already higher than so many of the other buildings nearby. Luca could feel his stomach contract.

'Don't you dare puke,' the guard ordered. 'I've already had to have one lot cleared up.'

Eban moved towards him with ease.

'How about you just focus on the buttons.' Eban said calmly. Luca was aware that he couldn't move. 'Look this way. Luca, look this way.'

Recognising his name Luca turned his head a little.

'That's right. Check out these.' Eban was pointing to the lit button on the panel. Every couple of seconds figures flashed on the numbered grid. The light was gradually creeping towards the top.

'It's just new that's all. Nothing to worry about,' Eban encouraged.

'How come you're fine?' Luca's voice was strained.

'Everyone is different.'

'How much longer?' Luca asked.

'Not long. Watch the lights.' Eban turned to the guard. 'Who made a mess earlier?'

'That is none of your business,' the guard answered curtly.

'Hey Luca, do you think it could be that big kid, you know the one who wants to sit at the front of the train?'

Luca smiled. He hoped it was him.

The light was slowly getting there. Ten away. Luca took a deep breath and blew it out slowly.

'You're doing great Luca.'

Five away. Four, three, the box began to slow a little, two, one, the box stopped leaving Luca feeling queasy. The glass doors slid open at the same time as thick steel panels in the side of the building opened and Luca ran to safety.

His legs were shaking but the floor was firm beneath his feet. Eban followed after and clapped him gently on the back. Luca rubbed his stiff fingers.

The door lined, airy lobby they had entered was furnished with soft chairs as if it should be full of people.

'Your rooms have been made ready,' the guard said not leaving the elevator. 'Choose your door, scan and enter. This is the competitors' floor.' The guard pressed the lowest button, the steel doors closed and Luca could only think that the box had slipped down the building.

There was a moment of silence.

'How're you feeling?' Eban said patting Luca on the shoulder.

'Fine,' Luca replied a little too harshly. 'I mean, thank you.'

'No worries.' Eban chuckled.

'I'd rather take the stairs next time.'

Luca took a quick scan of the space.

Eban could see no escape route. 'Hmm, not sure that is going to happen.'

'We're pris...'

'Shhh!' Eban interrupted and nodded to the familiar red blinking light coming from the corner of the room. 'So,' he continued smoothly as if nothing had happened. 'Which room do you want?'

There was no real distinguishing feature to each door except for the red or green light that surrounded the scanner. They all faced the circular lobby.

Luca was automatically repelled by the red. That colour now felt too linked to being under surveillance and he wanted to be as far away from the elevator as possible. So he crossed the room to the door on the opposite side and offered his wrist to the scanner. The machine beeped, turned red then the door clicked open.

The room was flooded with sunlight from the full height windows that stretched the entire far side of the space.

Luca squinted into the glare.

He felt overwhelmed by the extent and luxury of the penthouse suite. He had survived selection and appeared to be reaping the benefits of the prize already. Perhaps he was able to charm Tropolis after all. So why were the worrying thoughts that Luca had, making it so difficult for him to breathe?

Chapter 7

'Welcome.' A metallic voice echoed through the room. 'Dinner will be served at 18:00 hours. Enjoy your stay.'

Although Luca had been restrained with the food earlier, the thought of eating again so soon felt ridiculous and extravagant.

Extravagance appeared to be how they did things in Tropolis. This room was elegantly but not over furnished and the quality oozed expense. Again, nothing diverged from the basic white palette save for the steel fixtures.

Nervously, Luca moved closer to the windows. His legs trembled at the height he was above the city. He stopped far enough away from the edge and leaned against the back of the sofa.

The panorama was beautiful and terrifying. Tall glass skyscrapers punctuated an undulating mass of buildings spreading from the flat horizon of the sea on the far left to grey distance to the right. Tropolis was amazingly elegant and vast.

Luca had never really felt this small before. Height changed his perspective of the world he thought that he knew. Despite the impressive architecture, Luca was drawn to the sea. He searched intently for his home, creeping closer to the window, until his fingers pressed up against the glass. Maybe he was looking in the wrong direction, but no Outsider world was in his view. He had chosen the wrong room to be able to look back.

He caught sight of his own reflection in the glass. His father wouldn't even recognise him now. Angry and frustrated Luca backed away from the window and slumped down on the sofa. He didn't care for the fact that a large and luxuriously adorned bed stood proudly on the raised platform. He kicked off his shoes, curled himself into a ball and closed his eyes.

He would not allow himself to dwell with the Outsiders. He was in Tropolis. He was aiming for the prize, although he had no idea how to achieve it. The whole of the day's events seemed to crowd in. Luca couldn't help himself but go over what had happened and how he had reacted. The elevator and being the last to exit the showers came pounding down as massive failures. He felt he was the weakest, so much so that Mercy and Eban had taken pity on him early on. How could he prove himself strong when he felt so out of control and insignificant? How would he ever win such a prize as Compassion?

Being an Outsider had prepared him for at least one thing. He would not wallow, there was no option but to brush it off and move on.

He opened his eyes and stretched out. Someone was knocking at the door.

He run his wrist over the scanner and the door clicked inwards.

'Can we come in?' Mercy asked cheerily.

Luca ran his fingers through his hair. 'You got through?' He opened the door wider.

'Apparently so,' Mercy chuckled. 'Eban told me about the elevator,' she said.

Luca glared at Eban.

'Look mate, I've had a look round and I don't think there is any other way out of here. I thought Mercy might be able to help.'

'I didn't enjoy it much either,' continued Mercy, 'but I think it is best we work something out for now.'

'No steps or stairs or anything, Eban?'

'There are only our rooms and the one outside. No other doors, just the elevator,' he said patting Luca on the shoulder. 'Perhaps the best way to deal with it is to get you watching the lights again.'

'I don't want to think about it.'

'Luca, you've gone very pale,' Mercy said. She took him by the elbow and led him to the sofa, 'Sit down. Eban grab him a drink, the sweeter the better.'

Sweat drenched Luca's hands and his breathing quickened.

'We'll do our best to go with you. Stop panicking.' She handed him a glass full of bright orange liquid. 'Drink a little of this.'

It was a sickly syrup but Luca could feel the sugar rush almost immediately.

'You weren't the only one who hated it,' Eban said, swigging the last dregs from the bottle. Suddenly his face twitched, 'Yuck!'

Luca laughed. 'I know, it is isn't it!'

'Really?' Mercy questioned taking the glass from Luca. One eye closed and her mouth twisted and puckered. 'That,' she squeaked, 'is the most revolting thing I've ever tasted!'

Mercy and Eban sat across from Luca and laughed.

Finally, Luca asked, 'How can something such a wonderful colour taste that bad?'

'I was thinking the same,' Eban replied. ' What is it with these people? The only thing that seems to have any colour is the food.'

The wall opposite flickered and a large image of a slight but fierce woman appeared. She had been on the panel of Tropolites but had not spoken to Luca.

'Contestants. I am Commander Swift. I hope that you have found your living quarters comfortable.

'The first introduction to Tropolis is scheduled for tonight.

'No skills will be needed for this part of the competition but your presence is required in the communal area outside your door at 20:00 hours. You will be viewed by Tropolis via the Network. Good luck.'

As quickly as she appeared, she was gone.

Luca had grown up with the Network, but he had never seen any programs with the Compassion contestants. Maybe a couple of times a month the screens would light up and crackle with a message from Tropolis, often referring to a new law or restriction to the Outsiders or an encouragement to work harder for the populous as a whole. But, being starved of news from the other side of the wall, the Outsiders would watch.

Viewed by Tropolis. This was surely a test. He needed to be accepted by Tropolis, but how could he charm them? Luca's fear returned in earnest.

Chapter 8

The contestants had gathered in the communal lounge after a second message on the big screen had instructed them to go.

Luca fidgeted and couldn't settle. He was thankful for the calm of Mercy and the comradeship of Eban, but little could settle his nerves. The more he considered this test, the less fair it seemed. Commander Swift had said that no skills were needed, so how would they be tested?

There were enough seats for twenty contestants, yet not every seat was occupied. Thickset sat across from Luca, stretched out and taking up the whole of one couch. His confidence was unnerving and Luca avoided his glare as much as possible. Only seventeen contestants had been gathered. Two were now missing before this competition had even begun.

Small red lights flashed from the edges of the round space. Luca tried desperately to ignore them and distract himself. He began to consider the missing members of the group. Sniffer had never left the showers and another had disappeared between the food room and here. Luca wondered if they had even made it up in the elevator to a room.

He recalled the panel calling for results and giving him the all clear from the blood sample. What was that? Then he remembered the pin prick and the drop of blood whilst being beautified. It was his blood that had cleared him. This gathering was not the first test. They had passed the first test already; they were healthy. Sniffer was obviously not well enough and been removed at the outset and another had gone without even being recognised as part of the group.

Luca looked around at the various faces, his fellow contestants. Not one seemed particularly memorable or impressive, save for Thickset, but that was only because he took up so much room. Would anyone miss Luca if he were gone? He glanced to the side. Maybe Eban and Mercy would, but being out of the way only meant a better chance for them.

The silence only confirmed Luca's belief that this was a lonely place to be. It was no use wasting energy on building friendships when they could be snatched away at any point without even a goodbye. This was a cruel competition and he would have to win it for himself.

Mercy frowned at him, obviously struggling to read his fierce expression. Luca quickly looked away and sighed.

It was too late for doing this alone. He had made friends, the first he ever had. How could he return to being solitary when having someone watching your back felt so comforting?

A panel in the curved wall slipped away and a large screen filled the space.

All the contestants turned to it and saw the lounge and themselves on camera. Thickset began to wave and the screen version mirrored him.

Music began to play and then the screen showed a beaming male presenter. He was being filmed in front of an audience of cheering Tropolite people. The multi-coloured studio was brightly lit and everything on the set was sparkling.

'Welcome to the Compassion Prize!' he began and another loud cheer lifted from the crowd. 'Welcome contestants!' The screen flashed back to the lounge scene where the contestants sat quietly and transfixed. Thickset flung his arms into the air and waved enthusiastically. The sound of the crowd grew louder. Luca could not let Thickset take the lead so also began to wave.

'It is excellent to have you with us tonight!' the Tropolite presenter said as the cameras zeroed in on him once more. 'I am Nolan Smythe and you are live on the Network! This is an exciting night. The council have selected our contestants and now we get to meet them.' Another loud cheer and applause. The presenter made his way to the garish armchair, sat down and picked up a glass of purple liquid, 'So let us settle back and view the highlights of today.'

What followed was a rollercoaster of images. Each of the seventeen contestants had their original Outsider photo flashed onto the screen followed by the beautified version. Luca gazed at his image when it arrived. He looked sullen, scared and little cared for, his Tropolite version however had a smirk that made him cringe and a polished feel that screamed fake. His shoulders sank as the images disappeared. Who had he become?

Footage of the contestants arriving and seeing the large white building for the first time was followed by the beautifying. Careful editing had removed contestant 18 and 19 from the screen. It was only when the contestants were filmed eating that Luca began to appreciate the wisdom that Mercy had shown him. Out of all the contestants, Luca, Eban and Mercy looked civilised.

Up to this point Luca had known what had happened, he had been there, but the viewing with the panel had been a private time. Snippets of each contestant meeting with the panel were aired along with the comments made.

The last few minutes were taken with the contestants each choosing their door. Luca exhaled when he knew that the scene in the elevator would not be shown, but he wondered why. It might have made good network footage.

'What an interesting bunch we have,' Nolan suggested. 'Now let's take a look at the all-important numbers to register your vote.' The Tropolite image of each contestant was accompanied with a long number where just the final two digits changed. 'Don't forget, your vote counts towards the prize fund, so keep on voting!' The presenter winked into the camera. 'We will be back in the morning to see who is going through to the next round. Vote to save your favourite!' The final scene showed the lounge and Luca knew this was the last chance to get noticed so he stood, cheered and waved frantically. Thickset followed suit and so did a few of the others.

The screen went blank and the panel slid back to hide it.

Luca sunk to the chair. How could anybody judge who should be allowed to take part in the competition on what was just aired? There was nothing to base a decision on except maybe the transformation that had taken place with Franco and the other beautifiers.

Thickset said as he glowered down on Luca. 'What was all that about?'

'All what?'

'All that, look at me, I'm the best, little mister politeness and goodness.'

Luca shrugged.

'I've got my eye on you pal!' Thickset threatened then he stomped over to his scanner and left them to it. Seeing that the drama had fizzled out, the others returned to their rooms.

'I have to say the same, Luca,' Mercy said turning to him.

'I didn't do anything.'

'Except jump up and down, shout and wave at them!' Eban added.

Luca shrugged again. 'I thought you were on my side.'

'It isn't about sides,' Mercy said quietly, 'I just don't want you to be responsible for someone else's exit.'

'I'm not responsible for anyone but myself.'

Mercy sighed. Luca couldn't help but feel she was disappointed in him but he was certain he would do anything to win.

'Two people have already 'exited' as you put it and I had nothing to do with that,' Luca stated aggressively. 'They can't blame me for their bad blood.'

'What do you mean?' Eban asked.

'How many of us are here?' Luca began taking a calming breath. 'Two have already gone and I think it was to do with that blood they took. The first one didn't even make it out of the shower did he? They only want to take the strongest through to win. It makes sense.'

Mercy shook her head .'It makes sense but doesn't show any compassion,' she said 'Do you know where they were taken?'

Luca could hear his father's words sounding clear – the Death Room.

'I'm going to bed.'

Luca retreated to his room angrily. Even his new friends seemed to despise him.

He tried to recall all the references to himself on the screen, dissecting each comment or action, but coming to the conclusion that Mercy had made. He hadn't been true to himself and had deliberately pulled attention away from others. He climbed into bed, dressed as he was, and pulled the warm covers up. The lights dimmed automatically. He didn't care how they knew but was grateful. The darkness was comforting. No one could see him in the dark. He stifled a sob and turned over.

Luca stared over at the wall of windows. The sky was tainted with the soft glow from the lights of the city. Luca wished he could see the stars. Even the beauty of the glass city was lost to him as he contemplated the ugliness of the competition. Mercy was right again, when she had said that it showed no compassion. Taking the poorest of people and setting them up against each other. Mercy and Eban had shown the true meaning to Luca. They had helped him and guided him even when he hadn't deserved their help and they had done it out of kindness. Compassion was an action and not a thing to be won. Luca hid his face underneath the covers as vicious guilt bared down on him. He replayed the day, looking for a time he had good motives and was left feeling hollow. Even entering the competition was selfish, leaving his father to fend for himself so that Luca could rescue him gloriously at the end.

Weariness fell and finally Luca drifted off to sleep.

A heavy weight landed on Luca as the covers tightened over his face. He struggled to be free but the burden would not move. He wriggled and shifted, desperately trying to move his arms but they were pinned to his sides. He let out a muffled scream as something pushed down on his face. A moment later and he felt pressure on his throat. He couldn't shout, he couldn't move. Colours spread across his vision and he blacked out.

Chapter 9

A cool, damp cloth was being applied to his head.

Luca instantly opened his eyes.

Eban sat next to him on the bed and smiled down at him. 'There we are!'

Luca sprang from the bed fists raised.

Mercy tried to quieten him down. 'No, Luca!'

He didn't listen to her. The suffocating blanket still felt like it covered his face and he needed to be free from it.

The room was dimly lit but Luca could see the blossoming bruise just below Mercy's eye and gasped.

'It's all alright now,' she whispered. 'You're safe.'

He lowered his hands and relaxed his stance.

'Mercy, what happened?' he asked handing her the damp cloth that had been thrown to the bed.

She smiled and winced. 'Just thought I'd check, you know, as your door was open.'

'Open?'

'Yes,' Eban said, 'it seems you had a visitor tonight.'

'Someone tried to kill me,' Luca said shocked at the reality.

'And they would have done if Mercy hadn't come barging in.' Eban laughed.

'They hit you?' Luca asked.

'Well, he wouldn't let go of you.'

'I heard Mercy shout and got in here as quickly as possible but he had already gone.'

'Who?' But Luca already knew. 'Thickset!'

'Thickset?'

'The one who said he was watching me,' Luca explained.

Mercy nodded.

'That's the one!' Eban agreed.

Luca looked over and saw that the door had been made secure with a folded towel jammed in the gap under the door.

'How did he get in?' Luca asked.

Eban shrugged. 'But he won't be coming back. We'll stay the night to make sure of that.'

Luca's mouth went dry. 'I'm sorry.'

'Not your fault the guy is crazy,' Eban said.

'No, I'm sorry for being an idiot earlier and I'm sorry you got hurt Mercy. This is all my fault.' Luca got up and went over to the mini fridge. He grabbed a bottle of the orange stuff and handed it to Mercy.

'I don't think much of your apology mate!' Eban laughed. 'That stuff is revolting!'

'Not to drink!' Luca said. 'Just rest it against the swelling, it might help.'

Mercy sighed as she did as Luca had suggested. 'Are you alright?' she asked.

'I'm fine. Thanks to you.'

'What are friends for?' She winced as she smiled.

What indeed? Having never had a friend before, Luca was not sure. To put yourself in danger because a friend needed help seemed ludicrous. Yet, when he considered the situation reversed, he hoped that he would have done the same for her.

His shoulders slumped as he truthfully admitted to himself what he would have done.

'I don't honestly know,' he replied guiltily.

'You take the bed, Mercy. Eban and I can take the soft chairs.' He was doing his best to make up for his poor motives throughout the day, but even this highlighted his desperate need to look good. Eban and himself settled down on the soft chairs to sleep. Although Luca was grateful for their company, it felt like every moment with them that passed exposed another of his faults. He could not bring himself to send them away; they were, after all, doing their best to help him win. Yet again, his agenda was rotten to the core.

Soon the sound of slow breathing came from his friends, but Luca could not sleep.

Chapter 10

'Contestants must congregate in the communal lounge immediately,' the metallic voice announced waking the others in the room.

Luca was already awake troubled by his actions. He had sat up for the remainder of the night and had welcomed the new day gratefully as the lights faded in the city and the sun lightened the sky. He vowed he would endeavour to do better today, work harder to prove himself and be worthy of such friends.

Mercy's eye had swollen so badly that she could barely open it. Luca avoided looking at her, she bore his punishment and he could not escape it.

Eban tugged at the towel to free it from the door. 'Don't fret, Luca. We will stay close by.'

The lounge was full of contestants but there was no chatter. The low table was laden with bread and jams, fruit and pastries. The contestants were busy consuming the food.

Eban pushed his way through the crowd followed closely by Luca and Mercy. The buttery smell of the warm food distracted Luca from what was going on around him. He loaded a plate and moved away to the side of the room munching on the flaky delight as he went.

Suddenly, an explosion of rough laughter resounded through the lounge.

Luca turned to see Thickset pointing at Mercy, food spilling from his open mouth. But Mercy retained her dignity. She turned her back and walked away, head held high. Luca could not help but think that Mercy was so much stronger than he gave her credit for.

After only a few minutes the steel doors slid open and Crisp stepped from the elevator into the room. His stance as crisp as ever, but he looked angry this morning.

Suddenly Luca was not hungry.

'Contestants will be receiving the results of last night's networking in one hour. You are to be made ready. Follow me.' Crisp stepped back into the elevator.

Thickset shoved others aside to get to the elevator first.

Luca's heart sank. Thickset was not scared of the elevator, he was not scared of anything.

Mercy held back the doors until everybody else had stepped in.

Luca could hear his heartbeat pounding as he willed himself to follow. The doors slid carelessly shut and Crisp punched the button to take them down. Luca's stomach lurched as the elevator began its descent.

Grateful for the number of people blocking his view of Tropolis, Luca did his best to focus on the lights. He deliberately breathed deeply and steadily.

As it reached its floor, the elevator slowed and jolted. Luca let out a gasp.

The doors opened and Luca rushed out, relieved that he was on solid ground again. The steel and glass corridor was a welcome sight.

The other contestants filed out and stood waiting for Crisp to show them where to go. Thickset wandered over to Luca.

'Coward!' he said under his breath before moving away.

Luca puffed, not quick enough to respond.

Crisp walked in the opposite direction to the panel or banquet room, but the white corridors looked so similar that Luca began to lose his bearings. He stayed as far back as possible with Mercy and Eban. Soon, however, he realised they had returned to the familiar holding lobby and the beautician spaces.

'You are allocated the same as yesterday,' Crisp instructed and walked off.

Franco stood by the mirror waiting. He tusked and shook his head as Mercy went by to meet her team.

'Nasty bruise!' Franco laughed. 'Shame it won't help you.' He pulled out the armchair for Luca.

'She's my friend. You should be nice to her.'

'Ooo! Well aren't we all confident this morning!' Franco said as he began to run a comb through Luca's hair. 'Girls, get to work,' he commanded his assistants. 'Don't get me wrong, young Luca, I was only saying that when they have finished she'll look as good as new again. And besides,' he added quietly, 'the fewer contestants the better your chance.'

'I know,' Luca replied, depressed by the thought.

'Glad you turned on the charm! It is good to have you back,' Franco continued unaware of Luca's dampened mood. 'You did so well last night! I loved it and so did everyone I know. I told them that you were my one,' he added proudly.

The woman with the red belt approached. She took hold of Luca's hand and punched the tip of his finger with the needle. She didn't say a word and Luca was grateful for it.

A small drop of blood pooled at the puncture site. She dabbed the card to his finger and then inserted the stained card into the slot in the wall before moving to the next contestant.

Luca stared at his reflection as Franco began fiddling with his hair.

There really was no other way to gain the prize than at the expense of the other contestants. Luca would gladly see the removal of Thickset, but was beginning to feel uneasy about who else would have to leave in order for him to win. Each step closer meant that another Outsider had failed.

His reflection held no answers. The Tropolite that stared back at him was eager and would no doubt do anything to get out of the life that was his. Luca's shoulders slumped as the reality hit him. He was no better than Thickset. Another massive defect in his character.

By the time his session with Franco was over, Luca had sunk into a darkened state. He knew he did not deserve Compassion, yet he wanted it badly. Enough for him to believe that he was ugliest person there.

The contestants were ushered to the brightly lit and high ceilinged holding bay. The cameras and crew were positioned in the middle of the room, surrounding the large sofas.

Luca instinctively sat as far away from Thickset as possible, but this left him at the very edge of the group. Eban came to join him.

'Is everything okay?'

'Fine.'

'Wow!' exclaimed Eban.

Luca looked up from the thread he was playing with to see Mercy seemingly float over to them. She had made a remarkable recovery. Both her eyes were completely open and Luca could not remember which one had been injured.

'What happened?' he asked her.

'Lotions, and lots of them. I could feel it all tingling when they put it on. Amazing right!'

The healing had been transformational. Luca finally understood why Franco had said that the bruise would not help. The Tropolites were obviously used to healing their bodies and so a large bruise would not disturb them. Luca looked around for the boy that Franco had pointed out only yesterday, the one with the need for remedial work because of his complexion. Not one of the contestants had a single spot or blemish. Luca thought that the boy who sat three away from him was the one Franco had referred to, but there was no trace of any problems with his skin. They all had clear appearances.

Luca frowned as he thought about the lotions and creams that had been used on him. Even from the shower yesterday, there had been some visible effects to his condition. The realisation that the Tropolites had access to medicine that could remove swelling and bruising within a few minutes shocked Luca. How could they allow Outsiders to die of infection and illness when they had miracle cures?

Eban's sharp elbow shook Luca from his thoughts.

One of the crew was looking to their communicator. '... And so in a few moments we will be live on the Network,' 'What? What did he say?'

'They are going to announce the results,' hissed Eban.

'Five ... four ...three ...' The crew man held up fingers to continue the silent countdown then pointed to the camera which now had a red light blinking from the top.

There were no screens to view as the voice of Nolan, the garish presenter echoed around the room. 'And just look at our lovely contestants today! Give us a wave!'

They did as they were told, waving into the camera as it panned the group.

'We have been reviewing the contestants' first day in Tropolis. I hope you have been voting with vigour for your favourite because the lines are now closed, but don't worry, the lines will open again after the show to add points to their first challenge. However, the two contestants with the fewest votes will be leaving the competition today. The votes have been counted and verified. Let's see the positions of your top favourite contestants. Reveal the score board!' Nolan could be heard cheering and clapping, then he continued. 'So without further ado, would the following three contestants, who have the lowest scores, stand up.'

Luca was aware that all the Outsiders sat very still as they waited for their name to be called. They could not see the scoreboard, Tropolis had them exactly where they wanted them.

'Tilly ... up you get girl!' The presenter began enthusiastically. A tall girl stood, wide eyed and pale. 'Frank ...' A boy with spikey brown hair got to his feet. 'And finally ... Seth.'

Luca almost cheered when Thickset pushed himself up from the chair. This was exactly what Luca needed to distract him from his dark thoughts.

The sound of applause filtered through the speakers. The presenter was obviously in front of an audience of some kind.

'Now then. Tilly, Frank and Seth, one of you has been saved by the vote while the other two will be leaving the competition.' Nolan paused and the sound of ripping paper rustled. 'The one that has been saved is ... Seth.'

Thickset punched the air. 'Yes!' he roared.

Clapping and cheering was broadcast into the lobby.

'It is a sad time. We must say goodbye to Tilly and Frank. Thank you so much for taking part!'

Two larger men, dressed completely in white, walked towards the two failed contestants and took them by the arms. As they led them away to the only black door in the holding bay the chanting crowd could be heard.

'Death room! Death room! Death room!'

Chapter 11

The door shut behind them accompanied by the raucous shouts and cheers from the unseen audience. Luca could not hear the latch click or the key turn but he knew the door had closed with finality. He could feel the hairs rising on his arms and could not move.

Death room.

The death room equals danger. He could feel the heavy weight of truth contained in the notebook. The small book that sat unnoticed in his pocket had warned him and now he knew where that room was and the only way to escape was to win. It was more than danger, it was removal from the competition in a way that the Tropolite people loved. Did they view the deaths over the network?

Tropolis was not what he had thought it was. It was not a place of freedom, wealth and happiness. It was restricting, selfish and deadly.

'It is time for us to say goodbye to our wonderful contestants.'

'Wave mate,' Eban whispered nudging Luca.

'They will be back for round two - Connections. See you all very soon.' Nolan waved at the virtual crowd and then pointed directly at the camera. 'But don't go anywhere ...'

Luca could barely lift his arm, and he could not put together a charming smile to cover his revelation.

The red light turned off from the camera and the crew began to pack away. But Luca knew they were still being filmed.

There was no chatter from the contestants. Luca slumped in his chair. He pulled on the hem of his shirt as he tried to process all that he had witnessed in the last thirty minutes. Two Outsiders had been sent to their death while others remained overly well and healthy. Luca frowned as he wondered what the point of healing someone in the beautifying rooms was if you were about to kill them.

It felt like Crisp had appeared out of nowhere.

'Contestants are required to take part in the connections test,' he read from his communicator. 'This will take place one at a time. You will be called at random to the testing room and then you will be returned to your quarters.' He tapped at the screen. 'Luca, you are first through.'

There was no time to take any of it in. Luca tried to focus his mind as he followed Crisp through one of the doors opposite the death room that lined the holding area. He peered back. Mercy and Eban smiled encouragingly towards him, while Thickset grimaced.

The door blended in with the wall perfectly. The room was white, just like all of Tropolis but round with a stool and box with 57124 printed on the side of it.

'Sit there,' Crisp said pointing to the stool.

Luca was silent as Crips peeled the clear backing off the foam sticker before placing it on Luca's arm. The cold gel in the centre of the sicker warmed quickly as Crisp adjusted the fine wire that protruded from the outer surface.

Crisp's long fingers worked quickly, peeling, sticking and adjusting the wires. Each of Luca's limbs was fitted with four sensors. The ones on his legs pulled on his hairs and caught on his trousers.

Crisp reached into the box, pulled out a clear plastic bag and tore it open. He ran his hands over the stretchy wire mesh dotted with more sensors and then placed it over Luca's head.

He looked up at the wall above the door and paused. Luca instinctively followed Crisp's gaze. A high level window half circled the room.

'All readings are clear,' a female voice reported to the room.

'Last items then,' Crisp told Luca. 'These must be worn for the entirety of the test.' He placed the darkened goggles over Luca's eyes, secured the elastic over the wire net and then covered Luca's ears which muffled the sound.

Luca could still see the room he was in but the light was diminished. Crisp ushered him off the stool, picked up the empty box and left the room. The lights went down but Luca saw that he was being observed. The strip of windows set high into the wall revealed the faces of the panel peering down on him, the woman with the pristine lipstick, Commander Swift and the two men Luca had yet to hear speak.

'57124,' the female said loudly into his ears. Luca span round to see who had come so close without him noticing. There was no one there. 'Stand in the highlighted area.' He reached up and touched the headphones. 'Your test is about to begin.'

Luca could feel his heart racing and he was certain that the sensors were picking that up loud and clear. A small circle appeared on the floor before him, and Luca knew that as soon as he stood there he had to have himself under control. But his heart would not slow its pace and his hands would not stop trembling.

'57124. Your test will begin in 10 seconds.'

Luca blew out slowly and tried to steady himself. The test was named *Connections*, but how could he prepare?

A scene flickered onto the lenses of the goggles, cutting out the room.

Luca stood at a fork in a road. One path led towards Tropolis with its towering glass buildings; the other to a lush, green hilltop.

'Choose,' the woman instructed.

Tropolis had once offered Luca freedom. Yet he could not forget that they had withheld medicine from the Outsiders. The hilltop looked to promise life with the fresh growth and open space. Luca sighed. The plants were brightly coloured and swayed in an unfelt breeze. How he longed to actually be stood in this place. He could feel his breath slowing and his muscles relaxing. It was welcoming but he had no idea what lay beyond its promise. Then he remembered the black door. He did not want to be sent into the death room. He must choose Tropolis no matter what.

Luca turned towards the road to Tropolis and took a step forward.

The scene dissolved and Luca ached for the grass that he had left behind. Another image replaced it.

Two tables were laid out with all manner of delicious food. At the first table there were several Tropolites sitting politely, but at the second, the Outsider contestants, dressed in their Outsider clothes, grabbed and stuffed their mouths with food.

'Choose.'

Luca looked at the Tropolite smiles not reaching their eyes. They were hiding what they really thought of him. He bit down on his lip, wondering what conclusions they were coming to. What if all the sensors could work out what he was truly like? Terrified by this he turned quickly to the other table. The Outsiders were no different to that first time he had seen them eat. Thickset had gathered a huge pile of food in front of him and was now grabbing even more.

The choice was to stand with someone who had tried to kill him or to sit with others whose intention would be to kill him if he failed. Again the black door loomed. There was no real choice, he swallowed hard and stepped towards the Tropolite banquet to sit at their table.

Luca felt the test spiralling out of his control.

The third image presented itself suddenly. A large group of Tropolites dressed in white surrounded Luca. They were lined up in neat rows ahead, beside and behind him. He glanced at the emotionless faces, focused on something in the distance. No one paid attention to him.

The group collectively began to march, weaving past him.

'Choose.'

Choose what exactly, Luca thought. As the others went by he could hear the tuts and annoyed utterances. Luca began to walk with them.

Suddenly they halted. Luca continued to walk for a while, peering over their heads, wondering where they were heading.

'Choose.'

There was nothing to choose. These people were heading nowhere.

Luca stopped and turned to look at the crowd.

In a moment, they all sat on the smooth ground, cross legged and straight backed.

'Choose.'

From his perspective, Luca could finally make out the lines of people stretching out in every direction, each person evenly spaced and identical in posture and he felt exposed.

He was aware that he could be seen by everyone, yet not one of the neat people looked at him. He frowned and rubbed at his forehead and as he did so he touched the edge of the wire net with his fingertips. This was a test and he must choose something.

The blank expressions on the faces of the crowd assured him that they paid no attention to whether he was there or not. There was no reason to join in sitting or to follow after them. Luca stayed standing, he had no desire to be like them.

The screens went blank for a few seconds. Luca clenched his jaw, certain that his choice had not been met with approval.

A row of six differently coloured boxes were lined up in front of him; red, yellow, green, blue, white and black. They were about the size of his old rucksack, but shined pristinely and were sealed with a lid.

'Choose.'

Luca let out a grunt in annoyance. There was nothing to lead him in this.

Colour had been rationed since he had arrived at Tropolis, so much so that these boxes saturated his vision.

Luca thought that white would be the box of choice for a Tropolite, but even the need to win could not draw him away from the vibrant colours. He bit down on his lip as he thought. Then, taking a decisive step forward he picked up the green box.

He knew that this was an hallucination, yet he could feel there was something in his hands. Looking down, all he could see through the lenses was the green box. It shifted in his hands a little. The box contained something that moved of its own accord.

He set it down and slowly lifted the lid.

A hideous animal, covered in sores barred its yellowed teeth and growled at Luca. Its fur was matted and it stank. Luca quickly shut the box and stepped away. The box rattled for a moment then sat completely still.

'Choose.'

This felt like a trick and his stomach turned. He had to get this done as quickly as possible.

He turned to the red box and carefully opened the lid. This time there were large spiders creeping up the sides and hanging off the lid. His ears buzzed as in his fear he slammed the lid shut.

Before he could be commanded to choose again he peered into the yellow box. A pool of thick red liquid covered the bottom of the box and oozed out of a severed limb. Luca gagged as he pushed the lid back into place.

He stood, took a deep breath and moved on. He pushed aside the green box and its now very still inhabitant and reached for the blue box.

Sweat ran down his back as his trembling hands unfastened the top. A sustained hiss and a rattle began to grow. Luca bent down low and lifted the lid far enough to peek inside. A large snake raised its head, rocked to and fro then struck at the tiny gap. Luca slammed the lid shut and kicked the box away from him.

There were two boxes left, Luca knew he would have to open them too but he was shaking all over. He turned to face them. White and black. He shook his arms and then his legs trying to loosen the tense muscles. He didn't want to fail.

He looked longingly at the white box. This would be the choice of the Tropolites, but the Outsider in him wanted them to know that he would not be overcome with fear. He had faced worse things than dangerous animals and blood. He was stronger than they gave him credit for and he wanted to show them.

'Choose.'

He would choose. He lifted the black box from the floor. It was weightless. There was no way of gauging what this box contained. Nothing wriggled inside it and no sound came from within.

He placed it on top of the white box and took a calming breath.

He braced himself and then slowly raised one corner of the lid. No sound escaped and nothing moved. He lifted it further and strained to look into the space. He laughed a little as he realised it was empty. He stood up straight and relaxed his shoulders and took a deep breath.

Suddenly, movement caught his attention. Dark smoke flowed over the sides of the box and rippled over the floor where Luca stood. The mist darkened and thickened as it silently swirled higher.

Luca could feel the temperature dropping and he wanted to run and escape but all his muscles seemed locked in place. He looked about frantically for the door to escape the room, but he couldn't see it. He backed away from the invading gloom.

Soon he could feel the unmovable wall behind him. He placed his hands against the smooth plaster, dropping the lid to the floor with a clatter.

The loud noise distracted him enough to remember the lid he had held. He could barely see the box as it was being submerged in the thick smoke but he grabbed at the lid and lunged at the box. He twisted the lid and eventually it clicked into place.

The smoke disappeared instantly and warmth flooded the room. Sweat ran down his face.

He shoved hard, pushing the box to the floor. It skidded to the far wall.

Desperate for this test to be over he crouched down and opened the only box that remained. He wanted to fling it open but nervously raised one side. A golden glow filled the box. Luca's confidence returned. The inside was lined with soft gold fabric and in the centre, nestled safely was a crown.

Luca reached in only to have the image disappear before his eyes. The strewn boxes vanished and the crown faded away.

He sighed and slumped onto the floor.

A tall glass sheet that stretched as high as the ceiling with a thin slot at about eye level and a basket filled with credits materialised in front of Luca.

'Choose your score using the credits.'

Luca had never seen so many credits in one place. They would have fed the entire Outsider workforce, only they were in here with him and not available to anyone else. He wondered briefly if there was a way to smuggle them out, but then remembered that they were not real. Luca could feel the heat in his cheeks as his anger burned.

He threw himself into choosing his own score. Luca grabbed a handful of the credits and started to post them through the slot in quick succession. The glass lit up from the base as each credit was added. It climbed higher. Luca began to process what he was doing and slowed down. His first reaction was to give himself the highest possible, but what would the connections test be measuring?

Suddenly it seemed unjust to rank himself highly. He had failed to even understand what they had asked him to choose on several occasions so that must account for something. But if he was to avoid the death room, he had to give a score that would save himself. Perhaps a higher number would cover the fact that he had failed so badly.

He continued to post the credits into the slot, all the time calculating how the others would do and how he would compare. He hardly knew them, yet thought that Thickset would score himself highly. There was no way of knowing.

He had posted over half the credits when he paused to contemplate the Tropolite judges. They had created the test of the series of choices for a reason and would surely be scoring in a specific way. Would his own mark count or was this also part of the test? Was he to give value to what he had done? Luca picked out another handful of credits. He had done his best. He posted several more credits forcefully. But he had not been true to himself, Tropolis had yet again caused him to behave in a way that was not like him and made him feel ashamed. His choices had been based upon avoiding death. Luca dropped the remaining credits back into the basket. To give himself the top score would be another moment of failure.

'I'm done!' Luca called.

Finally the image dispersed and the lenses became dark again. The flickering light from a room that overlooked Luca caught his attention. A bank of screens flashed with spiking lines and flashing images while several silhouettes of people sat in front of them occasionally tapping them. Luca's room then lit up and the other room vanished from view.

A door opened to Luca's right and Crisp walked in carrying the container with 57124 printed on it and the stool.

'Sit there,' he said pointing to the stool again.

Luca did as he was told. He flinched a little as Crisp unclipped the box. The goggles were deftly removed and the wire mesh gently lay to one side. Crisp's long fingers worked quickly at removing the stickers from Luca's body placing them on a square of paper, before being thrown into the bottom of the container. Luca glanced at the room expecting to see the remnants of his test littered about the space, but the room was just as it was before.

'All done. One last thing,' he said handing Luca a small white pill. 'Swallow this.'

'What's it for?'

'The Connections Test can make you feel sick.' Crisp shook his head a little. 'That should sort it out and internally fix the experience for you.'

The thought of the lift back to his room made him feel queasy. He popped in the pill.

Again Crisp shook his head a little.

'You can go now,' Crisp said as he patted Luca on the arm. A sharp pain made Luca jump away from him and spit out the half chewed pill. Crisp did not seem surprised by his reaction. He bent down to pick up the container, standing on the pill and crushing it beneath his foot.

The concealed door opened, Crisp left with the container, nodded to the guard who stood waiting for Luca.

Luca took a step towards the guard as the room began to spin. He saw a white bed being pushed towards him. The room twisted faster, light and shapes blurring and sound became muffled and distant. Then there was nothing.

Chapter 12

Luca was roused by the metallic announcement. 'All contestants to the lounge in five minutes.'

Low evening sunlight streamed through the glass wall that overlooked the city. Luca lay on the soft bed unable to remember how he had got from the circular room to his quarters.

He could hear the muted movements from the lobby. He sat up and swung his legs over the side of the bed. The room began to undulate before his eyes. He closed them and took a steadying breath. His head felt like it had been beaten to a pulp and his mouth was dry.

His stomach went into spasm, so he ran for the bathroom. He vomited into the toilet and crouched there, panting for breath.

Luca could feel his temperature dropping as the chill of the air conditioning blew across his forehead. He pulled the pristine white towel from the rail next to him and wiped his mouth. He stumbled to his feet and ran the water from the tap, cupping a little in his hands to drink. It deadened the acidic taste but did not fully remove it. He then splashed the running water over his face.

Someone knocked on the door.

Luca took the towel and dried his face as he unsteadily made his way to answer it.

Eban was waiting for him.

'Come on!' Eban said as he grabbed Luca's arm to bring him into the lounge. 'You look awful. You alright?' he whispered.

'I'm fine now,' Luca replied tossing the towel back into his room. 'Have you just woken up too?'

'No.'

Luca quickly scanned the room. Most of the contestants seemed alert and energized, but there were a few that looked as if they were a little confused and had just got up.

Mercy looked exhausted as she leaned against the wall.

Eban hurried over to her, nudged her and put a bottle of the hideous orange drink into her hand. She quickly took a swig, shook her head and sighed.

The screen flickered to life. The female judge appeared. She had the dark red lips and had been with the other judges that first day.

'Initial results are in for the Connections test,' she began. 'These results are not yet finalised as the Tropolite public are yet to vote. The public will be voting and their results can alter the overall leader board.' Her lips tightened as she raised her eyebrows. 'The next test will be announced tomorrow, but in the meantime you are free to entertain yourselves.'

At that precise moment the lift doors opened and food arrived. Several Tropolite guards walked in pushing trolleys laden with delicious smelling food.

The contestants crowded round grabbing handfuls and loaded their plates. Chatter began to break out about the wonderful meat and the rich cakes to begin with, but soon small groups were forming and laughing together. Luca noticed that it was not light hearted humour, but often at the expense of some other competitor.

Luca had filled his plate, his appetite now fully returned.

'Do you want to eat out here?' he asked Mercy.

'I think I'd prefer somewhere more peaceful,' she said yawning.

Eban had filled two plates. 'Let's eat in your room, Luca' he said chewing on a chunk of bread. He followed Mercy and Luca into the room. 'Well, that was weird!' Eban said as the door clicked shut behind him. Luca raised his eyebrows. 'Since when did that lot become all chummy.'

Luca was surprised that he hadn't noticed anything different.

Mercy collapsed onto the sofa.

'Eat up girl! It will help.' Eban said handing her a plate.

Luca was concerned for Mercy. 'If you are that tired, why don't you just have a sleep?'

'I'm not tired,' she explained. 'It was that shot they gave me at the end of the test. I'm sure it was meant to make me sleep but I can't give into it. I need to be here,' She took the sweetest cake from the pile. 'You're right, Eban, the sugar will help.'

'It must be wearing off by now,' Luca suggested understanding what must have happened as Crisp had patted his arm. 'I'm amazed that you managed to stay awake at all. I don't even remember getting back here.'

'What are you two talking about?' Eban asked chewing on a hunk of bread.

'At the end of the test, after you got the pill, they gave a shot in your arm.' Luca explained.

Eban frowned. 'What pill? What shot?'

'You got a pill, right Mercy?'

'Yes.' She fished about in her pocket and produced the small white pill. She narrowed her eyes. 'Luca, you didn't take it did you?'

'It made me really sick.' He glanced at the towel lying on the floor. 'They said the hallucination can make you ill and it was supposed to make you feel better.'

'I have no idea what you two are talking about,' Eban complained. 'I didn't get any of that.'

'Why would some get it and others not?' Luca asked. 'Not everyone had been asleep by the looks of them out there.'

'Well it was given after the test so the only explanation is what happened to you during the test. What did you two choose in there?' Eban asked.

Luca did not really want to think about it. He had hoped that he had made the right impression, but it looked to be otherwise.

Mercy was open about what happened in her Connections test. 'I chose what I thought was right. The hilltop was beautiful and the view was stunning, it was a shame that it went so quickly. I ate with the Tropolites as they looked like they needed someone to chat with,' she said ticking the tasks off on her fingers. 'The next one was a bit strange with all that marching. I just wanted them to stop doing everything together, it just didn't feel right, as if they all were thinking with one mind. That isn't what we are supposed to do. The boxes choice was the easiest and the score, well I did my best so I scored myself high.'

Eban nodded. 'The hilltop was amazing! But I sat with the Outsiders. And the marching people, well, I wasn't sure about them so I just let them carry on while I sang to them! I gave myself a good score too, after all, I did what I thought was right. Which box did you choose?' he asked Mercy.

'White.'

'Me too.'

'White?' asked Luca.

'Yes,' Mercy said. 'White means clean and pure and untainted. It makes me think of the amazing clouds that float across the sky.'

Luca frowned. He used to think that white meant those things, but since he had arrived here, white meant Tropolis and Tropolis was not what he had expected. It was selfish, stark and empty.

'You mean you didn't open all the others?' Luca asked.

'You opened them?' Eban asked.

Luca nodded. 'I can't believe you chose white.'

'I didn't know you could open them,' Eban said. 'What was wrong with the white one?'

'It's fine. The white one was the one they wanted you to pick,' Luca said still frowning. 'It had a crown in it.'

'What about the others?' Mercy asked.

'You don't want to know,' Luca almost whispered. 'Not nice stuff.'

'Are you alright?' Mercy asked as she took hold of Luca's hand.

He looked down to see himself trembling. 'I think I've failed,' he said pulling his hand free. 'I didn't choose the right things.'

'They can only judge your choices according to Tropolite standards. Not one of them can judge you properly,' Mercy soothed.

'You don't understand. I chose the things that I thought would be Tropolite standard. I picked Tropolis, because I thought that was what they wanted but I wanted to go to the hill, I ate with them too because I wanted to fit in. I marched and sat, only because I was confused what the choice was. I not only chose all the boxes, but opened them too, I know that was the wrong choice because of what I saw. And I didn't give myself a high score because I wanted to appear modest, but really wasn't. I messed up.' Luca could feel the weight of his bad choices bearing down on his shoulders and he hunched them forward.

'Why?'

'I thought I was giving them the answers they wanted.' All Luca was aware of was the person that he had become and bowed his head. He had no excuses. His choice was to impress and not be true to himself.

'I wasn't asking why you made those choices,' Mercy said gently, 'but why do you think you have messed up?'

'I didn't give the right answer. What is going to happen to my dad now?'

'What would you change now if you could do it again?' she asked.

'I'd go to the hill.'

'Anything else?'

Luca thought. He wished he had understood the meaning of the tests and answered correctly. 'I should have left the boxes alone.' And he shook his head.

'Well then, maybe when we get out of here we will go to the hill.' Eban laughed.

'Get out? How do you see that happening and being alive?' Luca retorted. Eban shrugged his shoulders. 'Do you think the others that have gone are all right? It is called the Death Room for a reason,' he blurted out.

'We heard them chanting that too,' Mercy said sadly.

'It isn't the first time I have heard of the Death Room,' Luca recalled sadly. 'My father mentioned it before I left.' Luca took a few calming breaths to steady himself. He had already made himself vulnerable in exposing what had happened in the circular room and they had not mocked him. He was scared but thought that maybe friendship could mean sharing the load a little. 'Look, it's weird,' he said raising his eyebrows, 'but I found something a few weeks ago when I was gleaning. It told me that the Death Room means danger. My dad seemed to think there was only hope in the Death Room but he was wrong. There is no hope here, only danger.'

'Firstly,' Mercy said, much more alert, 'How does your dad know about the Death Room when we have only just heard of it? And secondly, what told you otherwise?'

Luca could picture his father in one of his dazes. His eyes would lose their focus and the only thing that would shake him from his world would be to talk him out of it. When he was lost, he would often mumble about things Luca had no understanding of. His father had only mentioned the room that once.

'I have no idea how he knew,' Luca realised frowning.

'It seems a very strange thing to mention.' Mercy said thoughtfully. 'Has he ever been to Tropolis before or worked here?'

'He's an Outsider.'

'I know that, but I've never seen him glean.'

'He doesn't,' Luca admitted. 'He's too ill. My mother taught me how to glean but she's gone.' Luca swept the air with his hand. 'I'm no different to anyone else.'

There was a moment of silence.

Eban asked, 'You said someone told you that he was wrong. What did they say?'

Luca cringed. 'It wasn't a person that told me.' He set his plate on the arm of the chair, took the large cream filled cake and walked over to the corner of the room. He clambered up onto the side table. He felt strangely fearful as he reached up to the blinking red light but was determined. He squashed the cake onto the camera. He jumped down, stooped to the towel and wiped his hand. Then, knowing that he was no longer being watched, reached into his pocket. He pulled out the small notebook. 'It says so in here.' Luca handed it to Eban.

Luca saw Eban and Mercy exchange glances.

Eban began to flick through the pages. 'You can read.'

It was just a statement of fact, but Luca felt threatened. It was a skill he had managed to conceal. He wasn't sure what Eban was accusing him of. He crossed his arms and just nodded.

Eban stopped at the page with the neatly written message and handed the book to Mercy.

'You can read too!' Luca exclaimed leaning forward.

Mercy smiled. 'Yes Luca. But what does it mean. Compassion, testing, Death Room, danger, rubbish hatch.' She continued to flick through the book. 'And what are all these numbers and letters?'

'Only the obvious, that the Compassion prize involves testing and the Death Room is danger.' Luca watched as they turned back to the number and letter combinations. 'As for the rest, I have no idea.'

'Where did you get this?' Mercy asked as she turned the notebook over. Her eyes widened and she gasped as her hand went to her neck in a reflex action.

'Gleaned it the day we got picked for the prize. And yes, I noticed that too.'

'Noticed what?' Eban asked.

'I know that you saw it too,' Luca challenged Eban. 'Mercy's flower is on the cover.'

'I wonder what that is doing there.' Eban smiled at Luca.

'That is so strange,' Mercy began almost tracing the flower on her neck with her finger. 'It is a Gibraltar Campion. My mother tattooed it on me when I was little. She told me the story of how this little flower was thought to be extinct but then a single flower was found and they were able to bring it back from the brink. It is extraordinary that it should be found here.'

'It's just a flower,' Luca offered.

Mercy smiled and nodded, but remained silent.

'So what now?' Luca sighed and slouched back into the cushions. He let his head fall back onto the sofa and gazed up at the ceiling. A blinking red light could just be seen through the cloud of cream.

'We can't all avoid the Death Room.' Eban said.

'We have to,' Luca began, 'but I'm not sure I have done enough.'

'It can't just be a coincidence,' Mercy said frowning.

Eban frowned at Mercy. 'Sorry?'

'The flower. I mean, where else have you seen this flower?'

'We don't see flowers! The heaps have no flowers and we haven't been anywhere in Tropolis to see anything. Mercy, move on, there is nothing to it.'

'Eban is right. Even if we did know what it was about, there is nothing we can do about it. Are you guys going to stay here tonight?' Luca asked hopefully.

Mercy gave Luca back the notebook. 'I think we should stick together.' And nodded at them both, resolute and focused once again. 'Try not to worry Luca. We can't change anything now and you won't be alone when the results are given out tomorrow.'

The door clicked and swung open and a guard barged in.

Luca jumped and quickly stashed the notebook in his pocket.

Without a word the guard clambered up onto the same table that Luca had used and wiped away the cream from the camera housing. He jumped down and stared at the friends. He stomped out, red faced.

Chapter 13

Franco beamed as he buffed Luca's nails.

Luca was exhausted. Sleep had not come easily and when it did, it was full of dark dreams and panic. Now it was another day with another test.

'My boy! Right near the top.' Franco looked over his shoulder towards another station. 'Just stay up there. I've got a wager riding on you doing well. Could do with taking something from Lamen, that cheat,' Franco turned and stared at another beautifier. 'Always complaining! Taken to whingeing about the recent admirable Tropolis initiative. Really!'

'I'm not sure how to stay top,' Luca said feeling more fearful that he would be sent to die and less guilty that Franco may lose his credits. He shook his head as he thought about how badly he had done in the last test. He would rather be distracted. 'What initiative are you talking about?'

'You know, lights out,' Franco began, 'We want to ensure that our beautiful land continues to be so, and by conserving energy, when no one really uses it anyway, Lamen,' Franco said making a face towards his fellow beautifier, 'After all, most things are charged up so we can use them. Not really that much of a hardship. As far as I know, the other sectors aren't complaining. The Network still transmits, we don't miss out. We can ensure that Tropolis remains the best place to reside by doing nothing!' Franco gazed off into some hazy dream then snapped back. 'Just steer clear of the Death Room,' Franco hissed.

'That is what I am trying to do.' Luca swallowed hard. 'What are sectors? You said other sectors weren't complaining.'

'Sectors? Don't the Outsiders live in sectors? You know, according to your job or status?'

Luca shook his head. There was little distinction for the Outsiders. Their only job was to glean to survive.

'Well, in Tropolis, everybody lives with other like-minded people. The beautifiers are all together, the guards,' Franco said peering around for inspiration. 'The important political leaders live in one sector and we live in another. It makes life easier. We don't have to socialise with others and it increases our competitive spirit, always pushing us to improve ourselves. Not sure how long it has been this way, but it works so well.'

'So you don't talk to other people who do other jobs?'

'No! And life is all the better for it. I can communicate with others who know what I am talking about. I don't mean to be rude, but explaining and talking to other people about what I do can be such a bore. Your presence an exception to the rule!'

Luca sighed. He wondered what sector the competition winners were assigned to, and if he would ever get there.

'Franco?'

'Yes my boy!' Franco was adding different lotions into a small bowl.

'What happens in the Death Room?'

Franco began to stir and laughed. 'It does what it says on the tin. It is the end of the competition and it all. Death.'

Luca could feel his stomach turn. 'Are you certain?'

'Don't you worry yourself about it!' Franco said patting Luca on the head.

'Do you see what happens in there over the Network?' Luca asked.

'Have you never watched the competition! Of course they don't. That would be far too much for our delicate constitutions.' Franco's eyes widened at the exciting thought but Luca was glad that his final humiliation would not be broadcast. 'But it would lift the ratings. We know what happens to them. They are, after all, no use to us, why should we support them?'

Luca was shocked at Franco's dismissal of human life. Even Outsiders had value, or at least that is what he hoped. But perhaps here, Outsiders really were just an entertainment to Tropolis and a passing of time.

There were definite contestants that had very little significance. Luca imagined the loss of Thickset to the Death Room and smiled. Luca agreed with Franco on this point, life would be much better without the likes of Thickset.

Eban and Mercy sat not too far away. Luca scanned their reflections. They were unaware of their worthlessness in this city to this people, yet to him, their importance in his life was almost immeasurable. How had it come to be? Outside, he had been so self-reliant and independent, but here, he had needed friends, and they knew that before he ever did.

The woman came and took his blood sample as Luca glanced at Franco frantically mixing some contents in the bowl. Franco had clearly not seen how hurtful his comments really were and had meant no harm. This was the condition of the Tropolites, this was what they had become in all the years while Luca had been gleaning for survival. Luca could not hold Franco responsible to this universal thought in Tropolis.

'We never see the competition,' Luca said sadly. 'The Network doesn't transmit it, in fact it doesn't transit very much to us as all.'

'Oh, you have missed some amazing years! Of course, this year should be the biggest and the best. But I don't know, maybe the Network has lost its touch.'

Luca sat back in his chair and let the comments roll over him while Franco smeared the concoction over Luca's face, arms and legs and rubbed it into his skin. Franco was not shocked by the fact that Luca and the Outsiders were cut off from the Network. He seemed to be content that society had placed them in different realms. Not once was there mention of the type of test that Luca would face. He bumbled on about the latest serum and the greatest trend in styling. Luca began to realise that Franco was a beautifier and not an expert, but he was Luca's only link with Tropolis. He hoped that Franco, with all his shallow interests and opinions, was wrong about the fate of the contestants.

The female metallic voice gave a five minute warning for the contestants to meet in the holding bay and there was a flurry of activity at all the stations. Fresh white or cream clothes were hung on the doors to the changing booths. Luca put the notebook in his pocket and zipped it up. The old clothes were taken away. Luca was sent on his way with a whispered command from Franco to stay near the top.

The high ceiling and bright light of the holding bay made Luca feel exposed especially after the comments Franco had made. He had no desire to be on display. He was grateful for Mercy and Eban's presence, even Eban's humming was reassuring. They occupied one sofa while Thickset took up the majority of the sofa opposite. A few of the older Outsiders had grouped behind him. Thickset glared at the other contestants in turn, but when he reached Luca he smirked. Luca pulled his jacket tighter around himself and looked away.

The cameras and the crew were stern faced and unfriendly as they silently adjusted the equipment and set a large screen where everyone could see it. Soon everyone was assembled. Luca quickly counted the contestants. None had dropped out or gone missing, fifteen remained. It was still a relatively even mix of male and female. The light on the camera flashed red then turned green. Luca couldn't help but recoil. Mercy gently placed her hand on his. The presenter's voice rang cheerily over the group. Luca cringed. There was nothing about his circumstances that could authenticate the presenter's mood. He knew the results would be coming.

'Hello Contestants! Welcome to the Network!' The large screen came to life. The image of the group was greeted by the screaming crowd at the presenters end.

The greeting was met with an assortment of awkward smiles and waving. Thickset waved in a casual manner easily the most relaxed Outsider of the group.

'We have been enjoying footage from your competition.' The image changed to a full body shot of Nolan, the presenter, sitting in some far off studio chatting at the screen of the contestants. 'It is traditional at this stage to have a little chat with the favourites but, before we can do that we have the highlights of the Connection Test to watch.' He turned to face the camera. 'The voting lines will of course be open, and your vote can lift a contestant out of the danger zone, so don't forget to vote!' The shouts faded away as the screen shot changed.

Luca gasped at the words. He could only hope that the Tropolites voted for him.

The image became one of the Holding Bay from yesterday, although, to Luca, it could have easily been today except for the group that surrounded Thickset. The footage began with the two contestants entering the death room. Luca felt the painful nudge, reminding him that he was here at their power to do as they pleased. He shivered. On the Network Thickset was celebrating as he had just managed to escape. Another voice began to narrate the series of events.

'Luca was the first contestant through,' the narrator said without much emotion. The cameras had caught Luca's frightened expression from what seemed every angle. Luca pulled his feet up onto the sofa as he watched. The cameras lingered on his walk down the corridor intensely. His hope for the Connections Test to be light-hearted was disappearing with every step he made on screen. 'Unfortunately, the test room cameras had a technical error and all footage from Luca's connection test was not recorded. However, Luca achieved a good score.' Luca straightened up, put his feet back down on the floor and turned to Mercy and then Eban. They shrugged and looked just as confused as he felt.

Luca felt the burden of judgement lift for a moment, but then caught Thickset laughing at him. 'They won't vote for you now! You're going down!'

Luca bit down on his lip and tasted blood which made his stomach churn. They wouldn't vote. He'd had no Network time. This had to mean his chances were slim.

'You got a good score, remember that,' Mercy whispered. 'And you are near the top of the leader board.'

'Don't panic,' Eban echoed.

The images continued accompanied by the narration. Contestant after contestant went through the simulations. The Network showed a split screen with the actual happening in the room and what could be seen through the lenses.

To Luca, everyone had done better than him. He backed away as each the coloured boxes appeared. No one had opened them.

Thickset, with his ever present confidence strutted to the connections test, but seemed to diminish during the test a little. His glare defied any chance that Luca had to rub his nose in it. Yet there were a few that looked to be in trouble. One girl who had her hair tied in a neat knot on the side, looked shocked when her connections test was shown. Luca heard her mutter, 'It didn't happen like that!' as she shook her head. He had to continue to hope, but that only made things worse. Someone had to go to the Death Room. If it wasn't him, another Outsider would die.

'So there we have it! Didn't they do well?' The presenter chirped. 'Let us have a look at how they scored.'

The leader board filled the screen. Names followed by their image. Luca scanned from the top. Seth, Eban, Luca. He was in third position. Thickset punched the air.

'Seth. I forgot his name was Seth,' Luca murmured turning to Eban. 'You got second. Well done.'

Eban leaned over Luca and took Mercy's hand.

Luca looked up at the board again. It took a while to reach Mercy. The picture of her friendly and real smile sat next to her name right at the bottom of the board.

Luca could feel her shaking next to him. 'The votes aren't in. This isn't the final score.' Although, he could not disguise his quaking voice.

'Let us see that converted into points,' the presenter began. The screen flickered. 'Now, the moment you have all been waiting for. The votes have been counted and verified. Who is at the top in your hearts? What are the final scores please starting with number one?'

The score board wiped clean. There were shouts from the crowd, but no distinct name could be heard.

'Let us see who are in the prized top two places. In second position ...' Nolan sat transfixed on the screen next to him.

Eban's face appeared on the screen. His image fixed into second place.

'Well done Eban!' Nolan congratulated. 'And in first ...'

Suddenly the screen flashed and filled with an image of Thickset. The crowd whistled and cheered, Luca sunk low into his chair. He tried to be positive about the result. If Thickset was at the top, there would be no reason why Thickset would try and kill him. The image than shrank and landed in first place on the board. Thickset sneered at Eban. Luca's temporary relief for his safety was short lived. He knew that Eban would be in danger instead.

'Seth!' Nolan cheered. 'Listen to that popular result with the people.' Screams and shouts could be heard over the speakers, but there was no view of the vast crowd. 'Time to find out where all the other competitors are sitting on the leader board.'

The pictures and names of the contestants began to appear in the rankings one by one. Third, fourth and fifth place were filled. Luca began to rock slightly and could feel the sheen of sweat on his hands.

Mercy's genuine smile filled the screen as she took sixth place, but she didn't smile as the results continued to flow.

Seventh, eighth, ninth, tenth. Luca had to swallow down bile. Eleventh.

Twelfth place. Luca's fake smile and Tropolite image flashed onto the screen. Eban and Mercy hugged him. Luca could breathe again.

'And so,' Nolan said, looking dramatically into the camera with a hint of a smile. 'Only one more space is available, yet three of you remain.'

A slender, blonde girl appeared next on screen, Clarisse. The final one saved from the death room.

One of the older and more muscular boys that stood behind Thickset crumpled to the floor in loud sobs. Thickset glanced behind and shook his head dismissively, disowning any friendship there may have been.

The last remaining girl sat perfectly still and open mouthed.

'Not Mirai!' Mercy whispered.

Luca could not celebrate his victory seeing the fear on this girl's face.

Mercy stood, walked over to Mirai and wrapped her arms around her.

The crowd from the presenter's end of the Network could be heard chanting the dreaded words, but Luca was focused on Mercy's act.

Mirai had grabbed hold of Mercy's face with both her hands and was hurriedly telling her something. In her desperate need to get her message across she had untangled the neat knot of hair. Mercy nodded in agreement and hugged her one more time then she reached up and reset the long, straight, brown strands in place.

'And so we have it! Are we all happy with the result?' Nolan asked his crowd and he was received with a resounding cheer. 'And look,' he added, 'such sweet scenes with the contestants. That's right, say your goodbyes!'

Luca could feel the anger rising in him at the sarcasm.

Mercy returned to her chair. 'It will do no good, Luca. Stay calm,' she whispered.

'Mirai and Zeke. It is time to say goodbye! Thank you so much for taking part in the Compassion Prize.'

Mirai stood with strength of poise. The crowd were chanting louder than before.

'Death Room! Death Room!'

She raised her chin and walked with resolve to the black door before any Tropolite guards could accompany her.

Zeke pleaded with the Tropolite men as they scooped him off the floor and dragged him towards the Death Room door.

Hideous laughter filtered through the speakers. Thickset joined in.

As they scanned the plate next to the door and it began to open. The temperature seemed to drop and Luca could see darkness seeping out through the open doorway. Mirai and Zeke were taken in and the door closed firmly behind them.

'Shhh! Calm down mate,' Eban hushed. 'What's the matter?'

'All that darkness!' Luca stuttered.

'It's not dark in here.'

'Through the door.'

The cheering crowd were beginning to hush.

'Luca, it's alright. Try and keep it together,' Eban said as he patted Luca heavily on the shoulder.

The darkness cleared and the warmth returned. Luca felt a drip of sweat run down his forehead. He wiped it away.

'And so, back to our contestants, for just one more moment. Well done! We have news of your next two rounds!'

The crowd were enjoying the drama as a white clad Tropolite strolled on stage with a large crimson envelope. Luca felt the prickles of fear. The presenter tore the seal and pulled out a card.

'In seven days time,' he began to read, 'You will be in competition against one another in tests of Endurance and Intelligence. You will be given time to train to allow you to be the best you can.' Nolan laughed and put the envelope to one side. 'Of course, we will continue to follow your progress. But for now it is time to say goodbye to you, our Compassion Prize contestants.' He began to wave then the camera shot changed and focussed on the group. The red light stopped flashing and the screen went blank.

Luca glanced at Thickset who had seemed to grow in size. Luca compared his slender form to the muscles of the other and thought of his dim witted responses to all the other tests so far. His chances of winning seemed to float far away as the Death Room door loomed ever nearer. Luca sunk lower into the sofa, his heart's pounding much louder than the memory of the excited Tropolite shouts.

Chapter 14

'This way,' Crisp instructed.

The cameras were being cleared away and the other contestants were moving. Luca instinctively followed. Mercy and Eban were speaking in hushed tones to each other, but Luca had no desire to hear what they were saying.

His feet felt heavy and nothing was clear in his mind except the crumpled contestant sobbing for the loss of his life and the darkness pouring out of the death room door. Luca swallowed hard as he tried to resolve to be strong when he was facing last place, but he had no idea how he would do it. He scanned the holding bay for another way out but with this many people, the cameras and Crisp keeping the group together there was no escape. The open space was as good as a deep, dark pit. Luca regretted ever going to the Compassion Gate just those few days ago. At least on the Outside he was almost free. His mind was muddled and he wasn't sure what was real and what wasn't.

Crisp led the group through double glass doors and along a raised glass bridge.

The sudden view of the city with its tall, elegant buildings bought Luca back to his senses. The sunlight filtered through the tinted roof and the hushed sounds of the world continued no matter what Luca felt. He moved closer to Eban and Mercy who shielded him from exposure to the drop below.

'You have got to be careful what you say,' Mercy said.

'I know,' Eban replied.

'I trust what she told me. Don't give them any reason to discredit you,' Mercy urged.

'That girl's Network recording was tampered with,' Eban reported to Luca. 'She told Mercy that it didn't happen that way.'

'None of us are safe. The Network is showing whatever they want.'

'Or not at all,' said Luca.

Mercy nodded. 'We have all got to be careful.'

'Somehow, I don't think that being careful will be enough.' Luca was certain as soon as he said it. He could feel himself quivering as the other two looked intently at him. 'We have to be in the top for the actual events, maybe those results can't be fixed, but the popularity vote with the Tropolites, well, that can be adjusted however they like.'

'Pay attention,' Crisp said standing right behind them. Luca jumped. 'I don't want to have to repeat myself when I give instructions.'

Crisp returned to the front of the group.

Luca, Eban and Mercy exchanged glances asking each other how long he had been there. They were not sure how much he had heard.

The group were stood at the end of the bridge. Luca strained to see over the heads of the crowd.

'You will be in training for Endurance this morning. The equipment will be available during daylight hours. Intelligence training will be completed after dark.' Crisp placed his arm against the scanner and the heavy door opened inwards.

Luca could hear the echo of the group shuffling into the expansive room as the door thudded shut behind him. Eye level windows stretched the length of the walls. The group spread out on a long line and Luca felt dizzy.

The edge of the platform had no rail and no steps. Each contestant stood some distance away from the sheer drop but Crisp balanced on the edge, facing them, with his back to the danger.

Luca shifted backwards until he could feel the solid wall behind him and looked up to the pendant lamps suspended from the ceiling.

'Follow me,' instructed Crisp before he stepped back and disappeared over the edge.

Several in the group let out a scream or gasp. Others took a tentative step forward to see the result of Crisp's fall.

'There's a net. He's fine!'

Thickset had turned pale but Luca could see he was determined. Luca considered that if he were to die here it would not be at the hands of the Network vote. He had a sudden urge to grasp back a fraction of power that Tropolis had stolen from him. He rushed to the edge, peered down and launched himself.

Luca tensed briefly. He fell through the air but he made no sound. He wanted to scream but he had no energy to waste. His throat felt constricted.

He landed in the net which flexed under his weight, but supported him. The sudden sound of Eban celebrating from above caused a bubble of laughter to rise up in Luca.

Crisp commended him. 'Nice move Luca.'

He hadn't given himself time to panic, but had simply taken the bold step and gone first, putting aside cowardly caution. As he lay back in the embrace of the safety net, he realised he had actually enjoyed it and his head was clear once again. There was no need for fear if there was a net to catch you.

'I think I could do that again!' Luca concluded.

'You will. That is the only way in. Don't expect any other soft landings,' Crisp answered.

Luca crawled off the net and peered up at the distance he had fallen.

Eban was leaning over the edge then suddenly he was falling. He let out a loud shout as he fell and landed awkwardly. Thickset's laugh reverberated through the room.

Eban lowered himself carefully from the net.

Moments later, Thickset had leapt from the platform and was somersaulting athletically as he fell. He landed with ease and strolled off the net with confidence pushing past Eban and Luca viciously.

One by one the contestants dropped into the net. Mercy was one of the last to join the group. She waited by the side of the net and helped the shaking boy who was the last to jump.

'Kit, you did great!' Mercy said smiling.

Kit was the only contestant that was shorter than Luca. He hadn't really noticed him before among the other larger and older looking contestants. His dark hair had been cut to give the illusion of being taller and he had a fierce continence in his dark eyes.

The high windows above gave natural light to the training room. There was, again an absence of colour but his room was not stark. Tall frames had ropes and ladders fixed to them. High balance beams and climbing nets were suspended between pillars but there were no crash mats.

Crisp's briefing was curt and to the point. 'One thing you should note before you begin to train - everybody has a strength.'

'What happens if we fall?' asked Clarisse twirling her blonde hair round her finger nervously.

'You get hurt,' Crisp answered. 'I suggest you don't fall.'

The thud of the heavy door from the platform echoed. Everyone turned to see a large and bearded man leap solidly from the platform, land on the net and then swing off the net towards them. To Luca he appeared to be an older version of Thickset

'You've not started without me!'

'You're late,' Crisp stated.

The bearded man pushed through the contestants and stood directly in front of Crisp. He towered over Crisp whichever way you looked at him. 'Get lost.'

Crisp responded to the rude order, but only moved over to a line of chairs fixed to the wall and sat down.

'I am Sergeant Atticus. I will be overseeing your training for Endurance. You will address me as sir at all times. You will be tested in each of the pieces of apparatus in this room,' he said, gesturing lazily. 'So make yourself familiar with them. Follow me.'

Sergeant Atticus marched to the far side of the room and through an archway.

Luca stared at the high wire and, even though he had been the first to jump, the thought of being tested at that height made him gulp. He followed the contestants, feeling his confidence ebbing away.

A large pool of still water filled the space.

'You will also need to master not drowning!' Atticus' laugh bounced around the room in a mad mixture of echoes, but none of the contestants joined him. If there was one thing that had frightened Luca more than heights it was water. As an Outsider, the boundaries of their homes were the waterfront and sea. It was a something Luca felt he could never overcome. Water kills. This message ran deeply with Luca, so much so that it had become part of his being. He was grateful that this fear was something that he would not face alone. Again, his dependency on his friends' strength made him sigh.

The Sergeant then scanned his wrist for the only door to open. Inside were four long narrow alleys with brightly coloured circles at the far end.

'The shooting range is always a favourite,' he said in a loud voice but it was muffled by the padded walls. 'The only way you will succeed in Endurance is to master all the disciplines. Instruction will be given by video via computerised tablet.'

Atticus opened a large box on the counter, reached in and pulled out a stack of battered and dirty canvas covered tablets. 'Watch carefully because I will only show you once.' He unclipped the magnetic clasp to reveal a dented casing and scratched screen. 'Switch on here.' He pressed a small round button in the corner. 'This screen is loaded with the video training you need. Each picture corresponds with the apparatus. To activate the video put your finger on the picture and it will begin. There we go.' A very young and fitter looking Atticus appeared on the screen. 'Place your scanner on the side of the tablet and you should be able to hear the instruction.' Luca could not hear the younger Atticus, although his mouth was moving. 'Tap at the top of the page to return to the menu then you can watch another video.' Atticus looked up. 'Hope you all got that.' He smiled with his eyebrows raised. Luca was certain that Atticus hoped no one had grasped it.

'The tablets are for you to use in the Endurance training and for Intelligence research. To access the Intelligence files tap on this icon.' Atticus pointed to a small picture which looked like a white triangle.

'But you will not be needing that until later, so it's best concentrate on the task at hand.' He laughed.

'You there!' Atticus pointed to Thickset. 'Hand out the tablets. I suggest you spread out and have a go.'

Thickset stepped forward and took the stack of tablets from Atticus. He quickly removed the cleanest and put it to one side before passing the remaining tablets to the others. When he got to the tattiest cover, he passed it to Luca and smirked.

'Despite what he says,' Eban said as Mercy and Luca joined him. 'I think the best way to learn this stuff is to work together. What do you think?'

'Best, safest! Either of those works for me,' Luca replied.

Mercy lit up the tablet screen. 'Where shall we start?'

Luca looked around. The contestants had spread out, not one of them had approached the pool. Atticus had sat himself in the large lounge chair as far away from Crisp as possible and was engrossed with his communicator. Luca was not surprised to see Thickset lingering in the shooting range. 'Looks like that one is free,' he said, pointing to the furthest climbing ropes.

The small group settled on the floor. Luca unclipped the dog-eared tablet cover to reveal a long crack that ran diagonally across the top corner of the screen. He sighed as he switched it on.

As Luca rested his wrist alongside the tablet, he could hear the narration buzzing in his ears. Although Atticus had said that this would happen, the closeness of the voice still took him by surprise. He moved his arm away and silence fell over the room once again; each contestant engrossed on their particular video, each listening to the different introductions and sets of instructions. Luca tried to focus on the training, but could not help considering what other technological secrets his identification chip held.

Mercy looked up and frowned.

Luca replaced his arm and started to pay attention once more.

One by one the contestants began to approach their chosen apparatus.

Luca watched little Kit attempting to climb a wall twice his height. Kit ran at it, brow lowered, dark hair pushed away from his determined face, but when he leapt his hands slipped and he fell straight to the floor. He picked himself back up and tried again with much the same result, before returning to his tablet, no doubt to consult Atticus' video.

Clarisse had managed to slide herself half way along the steel pole that was suspended as high as Kit's wall. A moment's hesitation, a sudden scream and she was dangling by her hands, with her legs kicking out for any assistance. Her arms did not appear strong enough to hold her but she managed to swing first one leg over the pole and hook it in place, then the other. Some of her blonde hair stuck to her forehead and lay across her eyes whilst the rest hung below her. She blew forcefully to shift the hair, but to no avail. Cautiously she shimmied the rest of the pole's length but had no means of getting to the safety of the platform. She grunted in frustration and lowered her legs but the quick movement was too much for her already weakened arms. Luca watched as her fingers slipped and she fell.

After a shout of pain and annoyance she got to her feet and limped back to the start. Luca was impressed with her tenacity. She approached the pole, the second time, having learnt. She lowered herself below the pole feet first this time. Hand over hand, she slid to the far end and then lifted herself onto the platform using her legs to steady her. When she got to her feet, she balled her fists and barred her teeth in a victory grimace. She clambered down and picked up her tablet.

The air was full of the loud bangs coming from the shooting range followed by Thickset's harsh laugh.

'Ready?' Eban asked punching Luca on the shoulder.

Mercy had already jumped high up the rope and was desperately trying to wrap her feet around the dangling end. Her hands were small and her upper body strength was not great enough to hold her in place for long.

'Just grip it with your feet.' Luca said.

'That may be what the sergeant said, but I have a better technique. Look.' Eban took hold of the rope, lifted himself up and let the rope drop to one side of his legs. He then lowered his far side foot underneath his other foot and the rope. He hooked the rope up below him and was able to stand on the loop he had created. 'It is much quicker and means you don't need to rely on just your arms.'

After a few attempts both Luca and Mercy had managed to climb to a decent height but now their hands were sore from the tough rope fibres.

'What next?' Luca asked.

'I think it is about time I learned to swim.' Eban said half-heartedly. Luca raised his eyebrows and Mercy took a sharp intake of breath. 'I can see that you both feel the same! We can head for the range if you like,' he suggested, with a shrugged.

Luca snorted.

'Watching how the others do with all this stuff will save us time,' Eban explained, 'but I think swimming will be my weakness.'

'Mine too.' Mercy admitted.

Luca shuffled his way over to the side of the pool. He dipped his hand into the water and was pleasantly surprised to find it warm. Completely different to powerful water at the docks, this was both cold and fierce. With a slightly more positive attitude he opened his tablet and began the instructional video. A younger version of Crisp appeared on the screen in the pool, in shorts and happy.

Luca, Mercy and Eban exchanged glances.

A clear and almost tuneful voice sounded in Luca's head.

'My name is Alec.' Luca snorted. Crisp could never be known as anything as human. He shook his head, trying to picture himself addressing the man by his name. He couldn't visualise it at all. 'I will be instructing you on the basics of swimming,' Crisp continued. 'Pay close attention, water can be very dangerous.'

The first instruction was to allow your body to feel the buoyancy of the water whilst holding onto the side, then letting go and floating on your back. Next came using your legs to propel yourself forwards then using your arms. Eventually, Crisp showed a neat and fast swimming method.

The friends changed into swimming gear in the changing area and met at the side of the pool.

Luca remembered how Mercy had been lost within the trench coat when he had first met her. Seeing her now, he understood why she could wrap the coat so many times around herself. She had gained some weight since being in Tropolis, as had they all, but she still appeared underweight and vulnerable. Her pale skin was in sharp contrast to Eban's rich and dark tones.

All three stood silently looking at the still water.

Luca felt just as he had at the platform when he entered the vast room with the hideous drop. Then, he just had to jump, here, all he had to do was lower himself into the water. There was no other option.

The ripples disturbed the flat surface as he got in and giggled. The water was warm and slowed his movements, but the sensation of being supported was releasing. Facing his fears head on was proving to be effective in overcoming them. Fear fed on uncertainty but the moment Luca stopped feeding it, he knew it would eventually die.

'You've got to try this!' he encouraged enthusiastically. He sank his shoulders below the surface and sighed.

Both Eban and Mercy tentatively got into the pool.

Mercy started by tip toeing, keeping as much of her body out of the water as possible and holding onto the pool side. She slowly lowered herself, her long hair floating out behind her.

Luca leaned on the side and let his feet lift off the floor.

'Have you done this before?'

'Not that I remem ...' Luca began, but then a memory flashed in his mind. He was very young, his mother was with him and she was laughing. They jumped over waves and splashed in the shallows. She held him up as he kicked his legs. 'My mother taught me,' he said simply. The rare, happy memory had been eclipsed by a greater disaster with horrifying results at the dockside. It seemed strange that this place would expose it.

As the friends went through the instructions Crisp had given, Luca found that his body remembered and it was only a matter for his head to get over the danger he was in.

Luca had managed to swim a fairly neat length by the end of the session while Eban and Mercy were still needing to be held afloat. Luca was grateful that he could be there to help them.

Exhausted and wrinkled they left the pool to try another skill.

In all they managed to complete several pieces of apparatus including the pole and wall.

Luca's muscles ached and his body was tired.

Crisp had already climbed half way up the scramble net when Sergeant Atticus commanded that the contestants were to go back to their living quarters.

Luca hoped that he did not look as tired as some of the others that stumbled up the net, but certainly felt that way. Clarisse hobbled a little, injured no doubt in her fall, Thickset and his band of followers climbed energetically, but having spent the majority of the time on the range Luca understood why they weren't so fatigued; they had not worked hard. But to Luca, the thought of Thickset knowing more effective ways to kill, frightened him enough to keep his attention sharp.

Chapter 15

'Best do these in order I guess.' Luca tapped the white triangular icon and a screen full of video links appeared.

Luca was relieved to be back in the penthouse apartment and refreshed by the energy giving food as they began to study for the intelligence test. They sat together, as Mercy had suggested. Luca would have expected them to do so anyway. She had said it was for companionship, he thought it was for security.

Luca knew that someone had been inside his room. A new model of camera had been installed. It was encased in a clear plastic hemisphere closer to the ceiling. It was not as elegant as before but cream would not be able to cling to this design.

Eban passed Mercy his tablet. 'Here, use mine. I've enabled the speaker so we can all listen together.' he said.

'What?' asked Mercy.

'Simple techy stuff really,' he began then continued in a whisper, 'They've blocked loads of stuff so that we can't use them properly. I might have a look at that later.' Eban laughed. 'Not that difficult really. It won't take me long to make all the reconnections.'

They all sat close together propped up on the bed. Eban opened the file and Commander Swift, one of the females from the panel of judges appeared on screen.

'In order for you to gain acceptance in the Tropolite community it is essential that you understand and become knowledgeable in the workings of society. This information has been approved for your viewing and instruction. I will not divulge the manner in which you will be tested, it is important to become one with the teaching contained in the following files. You must retain information and align yourself with it completely. I should not have remind you of the great opportunity to better yourself and become a member of true humanity.'

'True humanity! What are we then?' Luca said gesturing to himself. 'What exactly are they trying to get us to be? Become one with the teaching?'

'Let's just see what they've got,' Mercy replied gently.

Eban tapped the next link and a video showing the wonders of Tropolite life began. The narrator was poetic and deeply in love with his country, the government, the employment possibilities, the architecture and the creative minds.

'Are we supposed to remember all those people and what they did?'

After watching four of the links, Luca felt overwhelmed by the information he had been given but underwhelmed by any real substance.

'I notice they don't mention the Outsiders at all,' Mercy said.

'I can't watch anymore of this,' Luca said sighing. 'It's late anyway.'

'Ok then.' Eban switched off his tablet, 'Lights out!'

Luca laughed. He had remembered what Franco had said that morning. 'Tropolis is trying to get the people to conserve energy. My beautifier was telling me about a new initiative to stop the use of power during night time hours called 'Lights out'. As if they want to conserve anything! I mean, we see what they throw out and we know how much energy the Outsiders produce.'

'Well, that would explain how you got attacked.' Eban remarked. 'If the power goes off the automatic locking systems must be compromised.'

Weary from the day's exertion, the friends settled down to sleep. They ensured that the room was as secure as they could make it with the towel jammed into the gap under door. They knew that at some time in the night, they might not be locked away in relative safety.

Eban's voice was insistent. 'Luca! Luca! Wake up!'

Luca rubbed his eyes and peered into the darkened room.

'Eban? I'm trying to sleep.'

'You've got to see this,' he said as he leaned over and began to shake Mercy.

The only light came from the screen of the tablet laying on a chair by the window overlooking the darkened city.

'What is it?'

'All the power is off, right across the city,' Eban began. 'The security cameras went off too. Looks like they aren't linked to a separate energy source, but we can talk about that later. So I thought I'd have a go at restoring my tablet, you know, get it back so that I can access other stuff instead of just the training stuff.'

'Did you manage?' Mercy asked sleepily.

'You have no idea!' Eban said soberly reaching for the tablet and perching on the bed, 'It is all old technology. Stuff that I used to play with all the time Outside. But I've got it to connect to the Network. Had to jump a few passwords and stuff but there are things in the archives that I think you should see. All I did was search 'compassion', I was hoping it would give us an idea of what we were up against. And yes, Mercy, I know that is cheating!' He accessed a set of documents, much like the magazines and papers Luca used to find when he gleaned, photographs and video links. 'It's all dated so we should start here.' He tapped on a video link and a smartly dressed man appeared on the screen. This was not a modern white washed Tropolite. He was obviously a much-loved celebrity well-known to the audience. The set was brightly coloured and friendly and the host wore a casual blue suit. He was addressing the audience with familiarity and causing them to laugh. A small icon at the top corner of the video flashed with a long number.

'I'd like to welcome our next guest. He is one of my all-time favourite entertainers, now a movie man and soon to be political leader, Harland Barret.'

The applause from the audience was punctuated with cheers as a wild haired man entered the set, revelled in the glory and then proceeded to lounge on the sofa.

'Is that *the* Harland Barret?' Luca asked.

Eban nodded. 'The one and only, founder of great Tropolis. Looks a mess doesn't he? But he looks really young.'

The host greeted Barret. 'Welcome.'

'Thank you so much for having me,' Harland began in his very distinguished voice, pronouncing each word exactly. 'It is a lovely evening and you have wonderful refreshments backstage!'

To this the audience just cheered and laughed all the more.

For a few moments the two of them exchanged niceties. They talked a little about the new book and movie Harland was obviously advertising before moving on.

'Before we begin,' the host said smiling, 'let me first congratulate you on the birth of your son!'

'Why thank you!' Harland said. 'He is totally wonderful. I intend in having at least half a dozen mini-Barrets. They are all going be just like me in looks and character, because who wouldn't want that?'

'Excellent!' the host replied, although he did not appear to share Barret's enthusiasm for children. 'How have you been enjoying the fundraising event so far?' he asked.

'Oh yes, the event has been quite enjoyable. I have truly encapsulated myself in the wonders of the task of raising funds. I hope you have been taking part in the challenge that is hitting social media. I know that taking part does wonders for me and my ratings.' He smiled into the camera. 'Don't forget to peruse the footage of me. I believe you will adore it.

'There is, however, a matter of quite startling revelation that the audience may not be aware of,' he said turning to the crowd as if letting them in on the secret, 'but not all is how it seems.'

'What do you mean?'

'Well, the amount of hard work, pride and exposure that people put into something like this is not always gratefully received.' The audience was still playing along with Harland. 'I have, on my way into the studio, been spat at by an unsavoury gutter dweller. Now, these are the very likes of whom I have come to support on this show; a show for which the Network has graciously given time.'

There were gasps from the audience..

'I am terribly sorry that you had to suffer that Harland.'

'Thank you for your concern,' he said smiling as he turned to the crowd whilst dramatically dabbing at his sleeve with a silken handkerchief. 'And your correct concern it is too! I am sure you will be showing another video, no doubt very soon, to tug on your kind viewers' heart strings, but just remember that there are those that need to help themselves too. I hope that the money raised will not go to persons of the ilk that sit outside this studio. To tell you the truth, and as a political prospect these days, that is a rare thing, I am fed up with giving my money to unworthy charity cases.'

'I assure you, that only the deserving characters will get the charity we have raised!' the presenter added humorously.

'And I am sure that this show will be all the better for it!'

The video ended abruptly and switched to another of Harland Barret, some years later, among a large gathering of people.

'That was an archive file dated just over sixty years ago and was originally screened live.' Eban tapped the tablet to stop the next video in mid-play. It paused with Barret in an almost Tropolis style scene of serenity, he was laughing merrily with young girl sat on his knee. 'I found it among random parts of Harland Barret's autobiographical film that never aired.' Eban said. 'I thought you should see it before you look at some of the other stuff.'

Luca began to flick through the files.

'It is a bit of a jumble. There are records here that say that particular video was watched nearly seventy million times over the Network and his thinking quickly caught on. People were passing it on through a system called social media and using the Network to pass the message.'

'What has this got to do with Compassion?' Luca asked.

'It looks like the people freely gave to the poor until this event. There are records of millions of credits being given away to help people like the Outsiders before this happened. Of course, the Outsiders didn't exist back then. This was the normal way to help.'

Mercy asked, 'It was Harland Barret that stopped all that?'

'Not exactly. There are interviews and news reports that get steadily more like Tropolis today. From what little I have seen, he may have lit the match on what everyone else was thinking, because it didn't take long before the people were calling for charity to stop.' Eban replied. 'There was no one to run the fund-raising shows and ratings took them off air.'

'Not everyone surely?'

'No, but the ones with power.'

'What's this link?' Luca asked opening a medical document entitled *National State of Compassion Fatigue*. Luca read the title aloud. 'What is all that about?'

'You have to understand Compassion wasn't always a prize worth winning.' Mercy said. 'My parents used to say that compassion was firstly an emotion and the response was a need to help others.'

'This article says that the nation is suffering from compassion fatigue as if it is some kind of disease. It says that the Network had announced the growing number of people suffering had risen so steeply that they had been developing medical intervention through extensive testing,' Luca announced. 'It lists the symptoms as lethargy, insomnia, stress or anxiety when near people in a lower class, severe headaches, reduced work efficiency, frequent allergic attacks, stomach pain, chest pain, depression and over reaction. The list goes on. These symptoms could cover anything!'

'This report is only short, but there is a guy here who was sentenced by the court for saying that the poor need help. He was arrested for trying to give to the poor and a new law was put in place,' Mercy said pointing to the tiny section on the same page from which Luca had read from. 'This is the same year that Harland became the President.'

'What law? Hang on,' Eban said as he entered the series of numbers mentioned in the report. A new tab appeared on the screen. 'No persons may give away wealth to other persons without the exchange of exceptional behavioural and character references on the behalf of the recipient,' he read.

'Which means?' Luca asked.

'Compassion is outlawed,' Mercy said sadly.

'It doesn't look like the Tropolis we know was far behind,' Eban continued. 'The rich got richer, the poor got poorer. Loads of other laws are added at this time too.' He flicked through a few more headlines. 'The borders are closed, education and healthcare is only to be made available to those that pay. So, no schools for us; and no hospitals, and no way to get into Tropolis from outside. There are even reports on the building of the wall.'

Luca leaned back onto the soft covers of the bed. 'Not exactly the stuff they want us to learn is it?' he said. 'Harland Barret has so much to answer for. He has deliberately pursued and attempted to control us from that moment he was spat at. What an evil man! I hate him.'

They were shocked that the human ability to show compassion, in its true form, had been eradicated in a few short decades. The decline of civilisation had left the Outsiders without education and medical assistance.

The three of them talked until the soft light of dawn was slowly breaking into the room.

'You have to put your tablet back to how it was, Eban.' Luca finally said. 'You can do that right?' Eban laughed and began to tap on the screen. 'But don't put it back permanently. There is other stuff we need to find out.' Luca stared up at the ceiling as the long shadows streaked above him. A moment later the red flashing light of the security camera began to blink. 'I hope you are done because we are back on air.' Luca whispered.

Chapter 16

The muscles in Luca's arms burned, but he was not going to let go. The platform was teasingly near and he would have to push through the pain. He shuffled his hands along the beam, lifted his body high enough to get his elbow and shoulders above the drop, then edged the rest of his body to the top. He lay there panting. Sweat ran down his flushed cheeks as he looked at the floor far below.

A shadow fell, and out of nowhere, Thickset stood over him.

'Too difficult for a weakling like you was it?' Thickset said as he bent low and breathed in Luca's face. He leaned forward and pushed at Luca's trembling body.

Luca yelled as his torso began to slip over the side. He gripped the beam with aching fingers.

Thickset towered over him with a mocking smile. He lifted a heavy booted foot and was about to stamp down on the Luca's hold.

'Enough of that, boy,' Atticus said laughing, as he looked up at them. 'Save it for the Endurance test.'

Thickset stared for a moment, agitated by the instructor. He looked down at Luca and nodded. 'Endurance test it is then,' he agreed and walked off.

Eban dodged Thickset, leaned over and pulled on Luca's jacket. Luca struggled over the brink again, gasping for breath. He moved away from the platform edge quickly, resting his back against a solid post. He could not move even if he had wanted to.

Eban was busy talking to him but all he could concentrate on was the thudding of his heartbeat in his ears and his gasps for air. Unsurprisingly, Luca did not attempt any other apparatus.

When he eventually climbed down, he sat at the edge of the room and just watched as the other contestants continued as if nothing had happened. He was not registering what they were doing as his gaze flitted between the contestants. He did not feel ready for the test tomorrow.

He began to think about the Death Room door and what lay behind it. Then his remaining strength ebbed away. Was he ready to die?

The heavy invite with the Tropolis seal seemed fixed in his vision. It had offered freedom but had not fulfilled any of that promise. Perhaps his night time research had made winning the Compassion Prize an empty goal. He no longer wanted the kind of life where a society was based upon an attitude that only cared about itself and no one else, but there was no turning back and no get out clause. He had to continue. Luca felt weary just considering it.

For the first time in days, Luca's thoughts drifted to his Outsider world. He recalled the satisfaction of finding a great glean and transferring it to credits. The quiet and uncomplicated existence. He bowed his head. He remembered his father. He had not spared a thought for him and if he was surviving. Being an Outsider was just an existence but not a life. Only uncomplicated because food and shelter were the things of importance. Quiet because there were no friends and no family to share the burden. Neither Tropolis or Outside presented a more favourable outcome.

The slight scraping of the chair next him made Luca look up. He had been so focused on his thoughts that he did not realise Crisp had approached. 'You'd best to train, if you wish to succeed,' he said, as he sat down.

Luca felt unsure of being close to Crisp. 'Maybe I don't want to succeed.'

'That would be an unwise decision.'

Luca sighed. The decision was his none the less. Luca wanted to be distracted from his thoughts of Outside. 'Why is it you're teaching us to swim?' There was a long silence. 'I say us, but not many of the others have even tried the water.' Luca did not expect an answer and was about to get up.

'Atticus never bothered to learn. He felt his energies were best honed in the other activities.'

Luca sat very still. Was he saying Atticus had been trained here too? 'When did you learn?'

'At the same time as Atticus. When we were training for the prize.' Luca turned to face Crisp, but was quickly instructed to turn his face away. 'Don't look at me, Luca. Stay focussed on the group.' Luca could hardly breathe, but fixed his gaze on Mercy as she attempted the rope swing. 'You have to understand that you need to succeed in order to be free. None of you will return. There have to be winners and losers. From what I have seen of you, Luca, I think I could work with you, much more than some of the others. You need to be aware, that working with me is what will happen if you win.'

'What do you mean?' Luca asked as he bent down to re-tie his shoelace and sneaked a glance at Crisp.

'The prize is not what you think. It isn't what anyone thinks. You need to survive. I am confident you know how to do that.' Crisp got up, walked over to the scramble net and began to climb.

Atticus signalled the end of the session. 'Training for Endurance is complete. Back to your rooms,' he bellowed.

The contestants were escorted up to their suite. Luca barely noticed the lift, the strange looks from Mercy and Eban or the aches and pains in his body. He clenched his fists as he held back all the questions he wanted to ask Crisp. There had to be so much more to say. How could Crisp leave it when everyone was risking their lives for a prize that is not as it seems? What is it then? The more he processed his thoughts, the more muddled he became.

The metal doors slid smoothly open and Luca marched straight for his room. Mercy and Eban followed.

Mercy noticed that Luca was distracted. 'I want to go and take a shower, but I'm concerned that something is troubling you. What's the matter?'

'I can't tell you yet,' Luca whispered and nodded his head towards the camera.

'Eban, please stay here with him after what happened earlier. I'll be back as quickly as I can.'

After a short while, Mercy returned with a large tray of food. Eban went to collect some fresh clothes and then showered in Luca's bathroom. They ate slowly, waiting for lights out, which seemed to take forever.

Luca drummed his fingers: against the sofa cushion when he was sitting; on the edge of the bed when he stood still for too long; on the table as they watched the videos and while they tested each other's knowledge.

After they had enough of the sickly-sweet Tropolis teaching, they sat silently for a long time. The city lights far below gently seeped into the room, casting dark-shadowed patches onto the ceiling.

It was getting late. Luca could feel his pounding headache intensifying. He noticed Eban and Mercy exchange a worried glance. 'I don't think Thickset would have killed me,' he said. 'He'll wait until he can get points for it in the test. He needs to look good for the competition and as far as he is concerned, his ratings will go up if I get killed during a live broadcast on the Network.'

Eban shook his head in disgust.

'Don't you agree?' Luca said sarcastically. 'You've heard the Tropolites when the Death Room is just mentioned. I wonder how many deaths they have actually seen? Do they transmit what happens in that room over the Network later on? Don't you think they want something a little more graphic and dramatic?' Luca looked at them. 'Well?'

'What did he do to you?' Mercy asked.

'Thickset? Nothing out of the ordinary really.'

'What is it, then?'

Darkness spread like a ripple on water as lights began to blink out all over the city.

Luca explained 'It isn't him. What do you think the Tropolites are really like? We've not met any of them yet.'

Eban laughed nervously. 'We've been surrounded by Tropolites for days.'

'Apparently not,' Luca said leaning in to Eban and Mercy. 'Crisp said some stuff. He says that the prize winners work for him. I need you to look up past winners of the prize because he said he was one of them too.'

Eban gasped and speedily began the entry process.

'An Outsider?' Mercy questioned. 'But he is so like them.'

'Who is them though?' Luca asked. 'The only real Tropolites that we have kind of met are the judges and perhaps the beautifiers, but I'm not even sure of that.'

Mercy sat back in her seat and shook her head.

After a few moments Eban snorted. 'That's odd. Access is not as easy as it seems.'

Luca moved from the edge of the chair to the sofa where Mercy and Eban sat.

'Why is this information so secure?' Eban stated. 'I can get hold of the Network images for the winners, but that is it. There seems to be no video footage of their competition or information about where they are now.'

He loaded the photos. The screen was full of images of Outsiders turned Tropolite. Luca recalled his own Tropolite portrait and knew that the teens would no longer resemble their former Outsider selves. They were neat and clean and there were over two hundred of them.

'Well, Crisp can't be more than thirty five.' Eban said as he scrolled the images to roughly that time. 'That would take us back at most twenty years if he entered when he was fourteen.'

It didn't take long to spot him. He hadn't changed that much except for the fact that he smiled in his portrait.

'It's true!' Luca said, slumping into the soft cushions.

Mercy pointed. 'There's Atticus next to him. They must have won the same year.'

'That would explain why they hate each other!' Eban said.

'Oh, look,' Mercy added, 'there's the woman from the beautifying desk.'

Luca leaned forward. 'What?'

'And the guard that took us up in the elevator,' Eban laughed. 'Nice jacket! Oh, there are quite a few of the guards on here. Even some of the older winners.'

'Is Franco there or any of the beautifiers?' Luca asked.

'I can't see Eva,' Mercy said scanning the images. 'And I don't recognise any of the others there.'

Luca slouched again. 'I guess Crisp was telling the truth about that.' Luca turned away from the screen and bit down on his lip.

'There is something you're not telling us. Luca, what is it?' She stared at him, encouraging a reply.

Luca sighed. 'Crisp said the competition is not what anyone thinks it is.' Luca turned to face his friends. 'Do you think their families were sent for when they won?'

Mercy shrugged her shoulders sadly.

'I can't tell from the files,' Eban said. 'They just don't seem to exist.'

'What is the competition about, then?' Luca asked rubbing his hand over his face. 'What is the point of winning?'

'You need to remember where you have come from, Luca.' Mercy said, almost sternly. 'Outsiders are struggling to survive but you are here, with the chance to change that.'

'What can I do to change that?' Luca said, his face getting hot. 'I am a nothing, both here and there.'

'You are not a nothing. What a lie!' Mercy was close to tears. 'You're our friend.'

Luca had always thought of himself as a nothing. He had no real family, no life and just scraped an existence. For all these years he had built his life on the firm foundation that he didn't matter in the grand scheme of things. But if Mercy was right, if he really did have value and that it was somehow fated to this competition, he was not a nothing.

'There has to be something that we can change,' Mercy said. 'The prize may not be what we expected but Crisp seems to have made something of himself. We have to find the prize for ourselves. It may not be what we were expecting but it can be better than that. It has to be better than that.'

They all sat in silence.

'What do we do?' Luca asked in a small voice.

'We have to break the divide between the Outsiders and Tropolis.'

Eban laughed breaking the tension. 'I love the simplicity of the plan, Mercy!'

'I have no plan!' Mercy said beginning to giggle as she looked at the tablet and began to hover the icon over the images.

'Well, let's think it through,' Luca said. 'We need to know what we are up against, right? We need to know all there is to know about how to win this. When one of us wins, then we will have some influence.' Luca tried to put to the back of his mind that there were only two winners. Instead, he thought of their possibilities and decided that gave them, as a circle of friends, a good chance. 'We need them for freedom, but they must need us for something too.'

'You're right,' Eban said. 'They need the Outsiders to get electric power to their city! That's something that they seem to be lacking right now. Here, throw this in the bin.' Eban handed Luca an unwrapped cake.

'What's the matter with that?'

'Nothing! That's why I want my fellow Outsiders to have a taste!'

Luca began to smile. 'Yes! It'll get to them eventually! What Tropolis doesn't want gets thrown away like rubbish. We could feed a few of them from here, but not nearly enough.'

'Small beginnings,' Eban said with a smile, 'can lead to big changes. We saw that from that chat show the other night.'

Mercy started, as if she had suddenly noticed something important, and didn't want the moment to pass. 'What did you say?'

'The chat show, the one with Harland Barret.'

'No, what did Luca say?'

Luca shrugged. 'I don't know. Something about throwing our rubbish to the Outsiders not being enough?'

'Rubbish!' Mercy looked up at Luca. 'Where's that notebook?'

Luca pulled out the notebook from his pocket.

Mercy opened to what seemed a random page and laughed. 'I thought I'd seen numbers like this before. They're dates. All this column! It's a list of dates.'

Luca didn't grasp the connection. 'What? How did you get that from talking about rubbish?'

'The photos have dates on them. Look.' She placed the icon over the picture of Crisp and a six digit number with details of the image flashed up. 'You reminded me of the numbers in the book before the message about the rubbish hatch.'

'Keep the book open there,' Eban said, as he typed the series of numbers into a page full of code. Several documents flashed onto the screen. Eban flicked through them quickly but stopped at one with the Tropolis crest at the top. He began to hum. He then accessed the coded page again and replaced the numbers with another set from the notebook. Again, several more pages opened. He continued this process a few more times.

Luca watched, fascinated, but unenlightened. 'Er, Eban?'

'Yep.'

'What is it?'

Eban took a deep breath. 'They are dates. All of them are dates. And some are quite recent. You see this column next to them? Well, they're people. Look.' Eban didn't give the others a chance to study the information before he continued. 'The people in this document are a list of missing persons. See their names? The initials are the same as the letters next to the dates they went missing.' He jabbed his finger to the corresponding code in the notebook. 'The last four numbers I'm guessing are times. They would work as a clock right? It occurs for these six entries. My guess is it would match up for all the rest too.'

'What happened to the people that went missing?'

Eban entered new searches using the names he had found. 'Dead. At least that is what the news articles say. The Tropolis files don't make a further entry. Still missing then, I suppose.'

Mercy asked 'How could you go missing in a city like Tropolis?'

Wherever you went you were scanned. Tropolis knew exactly where everyone was. Luca shook his head. There was nowhere to go.

Chapter 17

Luca knew that he needed to rest to restore his energy, but his mind would not settle, no matter how long he waited. He had remained as quiet and as still as he could while his friends slept, but as soon as the morning light began to break over the city he got up, paced for a while. He tore a small bunch of grapes from the cluster in the bowl, then sat on the floor by the window. He pulled off some grapes and popped them into his mouth.

He had been so fearful of heights when he had first entered Tropolis, but now the elevation was comforting. Somehow, it reflected his changing perspective on of all the things he had once believed.

He no longer despised the life Outside and his longing for Tropolis had been eradicated. Being Outside contained its own barriers but Tropolis was full of boundaries and expectations that could never be met fully. The Compassion Prize tests had confirmed that not one of the Outsiders would be exactly what Tropolis desired.

Luca now regarded having other people in his life as a blessing rather than a curse. It was possible to have value even when you failed and messed up; his friends had taught him that.

His worth was not contained in what he could do, but who he was.

He pulled up his knees, rested his chin on them and sighed. His breath clouded the glass.

Then there were questions with regard to Crisp, the prize and the security of the contestants. It was these things that troubled him most. Luca doodled a single leaf in the misted glass. He hastily wiped it away.

The sun persistently flooded the landscape with heat and no doubt raised a stench in the heaps Outside. Bright sunlight streamed over the city but Tropolis had lost its gleam and sparkle. It was a place of death, not only for the body if you lost in the competition, but Luca could feel it killing him from the inside with each test. Quietly, in the stillness of his room, Luca searched for a little hope.

He twiddled the empty grape stalk between his fingers. Then a thought splashed into his mind.

People had left and not been found. People had escaped Tropolis. If they could, so could he. He glanced over at his friends sleeping. So could Eban and Mercy. But how?

The notebook had faithfully recorded those that had left.

Warmth flooded over him.

'That's it!' he muttered as he lifted his head. 'Please. Please, that has got to be it.' There had to be a way out and he had the answer with him all this time. The notebook had warned of the Death Room, it had even been clear that the Compassion Prize was about testing. It had contained the details of the missing or escaped people from Tropolis and it held one more clue.

Luca stared at the redundant stalk.

With all the doors. corridors and cameras in this building, there appeared to be no way out, but one thing was always removed and sent to the Outside: the rubbish. The way to escape was to be sent away with the rubbish. After all, the notebook, an obvious item sent from Tropolis had made it to the heaps, it had been deposited and found. And now it would be put to good use.

Luca got to his feet and turned, ready to wake his friends and formulate a plan, but he caught sight of the blinking red light of the security camera. He would have to wait until it was safe to do so. He dropped the stalk into the rubbish bin and then tucked his hand into his pocket where the notebook was hidden. He approached the glass wall and stared at the grey sheen of dirt highlighted by the sun's rays on the external glass.

'All contestants must collect their Endurance Test uniforms and meet in the lobby in ten minutes,' the metallic female voice announced. Luca started and banged his head against the glass. He was exhausted having not really slept.

Eban, Mercy and Luca collected their clothes and changed into the soft fabrics. For the first time since they had entered Tropolis, they were issued with coloured t-shirts to go along with their white shorts. Eban wore orange and Mercy dressed in purple, each with their name emblazoned on their backs. Luca felt a little uneasy about his blue shirt but put that down to nerves. The shoes were pliable, with very thin rubberised soles.

Luca wanted to speak to his friends, but they would be seen and possibly overheard if he did. He clenched his teeth in frustration.

When all the contestants gathered in the communal lounge, Luca's stomach began to tighten.

The lift arrived and the guards gathered half the group and descended.

Luca, Eban and Mercy were left with Kit, the dark haired boy Mercy had encouraged to jump into the net in training, and Clarisse, who still hobbled a little on her hurt ankle. It was a few moments before Luca realised that Thickset and another girl, whose wild, curly hair framed her face like a mane stood at the far side of the room. Thickset's red t-shirt stretched tightly over his defined muscles – a look he seemed very pleased with. Luca had not been aware of his opponent's threatening, physical change until now. Luca shivered.

He remained alert. He was not focused on Mercy's friendly conversation with Kit and Clarisse. A nervous giggle emerged from the chatter and caught the attention of Thickset who found Luca staring at him.

Luca shuffled back towards the wall.

'You see that worm, Danita?' Thickset said loudly to the bushy haired girl.

'Only just, Seth!' she mocked, squinting in Luca's direction. 'He is so small. I think he has had a lucky streak getting this far.' She laughed, tilting her head back and exposing her whitened teeth.

Her physique was slender and more athletic than the other girls, and she looked to be a couple of years older. Her shirt was a dark blue. Luca automatically flattened his own lighter blue t-shirt as he felt the tension growing. He could not trust anyone who would associate themselves with Thickset.

'Well that worm,' Thickset began as he pushed himself off the wall and slowly approached, 'is going to die today.'

Luca's heart raced.

'What's the matter?' Thickset asked.' You going to hide behind them again?'

Luca's hands were slick against the wall. 'I'm not hiding,' Luca said quietly.

Thickset laughed. ' Tropolis needs real men, and you will never be one of them.'

Eban asked full of confidence. 'And just what do you think is a real man?' He didn't wait for a reply. 'I don't think real men need to prove themselves the way you are suggesting.'

'Who asked you?' Thickset hissed prodding Eban in the chest. 'Tropolis knows the best way to sort out the men from the worms.' He pushed Eban to one side and moved uncomfortably close to Luca. 'So, what kind of death would you like?' Thickset said breathing in Luca's face.

Painless, quick were his first thoughts, but Luca knew he had to get through Endurance. 'Not today,' he said.

'What did you say?'

'Not today. I'm not going to die today.'

Thickset's face started to redden and he began to scowl. His hand tightened around Luca's throat and suddenly, Luca was struggling for air. Dark spots began to swim his vision. He could hear Mercy shouting and felt his head being shaken before he was dropped on the ground.

Cool air poured through his bruised airway as he slumped to the floor unable to hold himself upright.

'Enough!' shouted Crisp as he grabbed the back of Thickset's shirt and pulled him away. 'Save it for the test. Get him out of here,' he instructed the guards. 'All of you get going!'

Luca looked up to see Danita guiding Thickset towards the lift followed closely by the others. Mercy's hair was dishevelled, her face was flushed and she gritted her teeth. Eban stood between her and Thickset before the lift doors closed.

Crisp bent down to Luca and helped him to his feet. Without a word Crisp took him to the sofa and sat him down. He went into Luca's room and emerged a few minutes later with an ice filled cloth and a drink.

Luca took the offered cup and swallowed painfully.

Crisp sat down next to him. 'What do you think you were doing?' he asked.

'Nothing,' croaked Luca defensively holding the cloth against the bruising.

'You should be conserving your energy.'

Luca drank some more liquid which burned his throat.

They both sat in silence. Luca tried to steady his shaking hands.

'You need to focus on the task,' Crisp instructed quietly bringing his hands together in front of him as if directing.

'Excuse me while I just recover from nearly being killed for the second time.'

'Are you angry with me?' Crisp finally looked at Luca. 'Because you need to direct that somewhere else.'

Luca frowned shook his head.

'I did not put you here,' Crisp stated.

'But you don't appear to be helping me out either.' Luca tentatively touched his throat. 'Don't worry about me. I'll focus on the test and maybe I'll survive another day.' Luca stood quickly.

Crisp sighed. 'You have it all wrong if you think I am not helping you.' Crisp got to his feet – a much grander gesture because of his height. 'You know nothing about my motivations. You should be grateful that there is someone from Tropolis looking out for you Luca, despite being an Outsider.'

'Despite you being an Outsider you mean! You know that death lies in store for us, yet you continue to work for them.' Luca marched over to the lift and punched the call button. 'You aren't helping anyone but yourself.'

'You chose to be here Luca.'

'What I chose was a free life, but I can't get that here,' Luca stated and Crisp seemed to slump a little at his words. 'I don't think that working for Tropolis is freedom at all, especially if it means sending my own people to death. I may have made a choice to enter the competition, just as you did, but this was not what was promised.'

Luca could hear the whirring of the elevator motor.

'Nothing was ever promised only implied,' Crisp said. 'What you thought you were getting was never on the agenda.'

'The only thing on the agenda is your precious Tropolis destroying the Outsiders from both sides of the wall.'

Crisp walked across the lobby and stood very close. He bent down. 'Tropolis is not precious to me,' he whispered and Luca huffed out a little laugh. 'Don't, for one minute, think that I am unconcerned about what happens in this building to the people who are my history.' Crisp paused. Luca dared not look at his face. 'I care much more then you think.' His voice quivered a little and then he took a deep breath.

Luca chanced a quick glance, certain he wanted to see this man crumbling. He wanted Crisp to say more. Instead, the Tropolite stood upright and straightened his jacket.

'Focus your emotions, Luca. Use them as an impetus to get you through to the next round.'

The lift doors opened. Crisp stepped inside and Luca joined him.

'But we both know that results can be modified,' Luca said.

'Not in this task. You won't be able to blame anyone but yourself if you lose.'

Chapter 18

The black veined marble floor and high, glass ceiling bounced the voices of the contestants around the space. The echoes were muddled, confusing, and loud in Luca's ears. He had endured the uncomfortable silence of the enclosed elevator, hardly noticing the drop to the lowest level. The rest of the group had been ushered through a heavy door, looked to be part of the wall, when it was sealed. Crisp directed Luca without a word.

Luca could not fail to marvel at the beauty of the space, the elegant steels, sparking glass and piercing light. The scene was familiar. He peered to one side and saw the frosted glass doors that led to the cleaning rooms that had removed his Outsider identity. The space suddenly felt tainted. The light was too bright and the structure was falsely simplistic.

Luca caught Eban's concerning gaze. He shook his head and tried to push his hands into his pockets but his shorts had none. He folded his arms and puffed out some air.

'Follow me!' Crisp instructed in a monotone voice and marched over to the stairwell followed by the guards.

The group bustled into action. Thickset, with his followers taking the lead; Mercy, Eban and Luca trailed behind.

'You alright?' Eban asked.

'Fine,' Luca snapped. 'Let's just get through this.'

Luca saw the exchanged glance between Mercy and Eban but said nothing more.

The gentle taps of the contestants' feet filled the space as they sped down the stairs. The cool air of the world above faded as the warmer, slightly greasy air replaced it. Deeper into the ground they zigzagged until a large sweeping arch marked their arrival at the station.

The mirrored, vaulted ceiling reflected the group. Luca remembered the apprehensive faces from before; now they had changed. There was expectancy and fear. Luca's breathing became shallow. He wiped his sweaty hands over his shorts. He dared to look up. His own reflection frightened him the most. He no longer saw the Outsider, but neither did he see the Tropolite. He could not convince himself of belonging to either place. Others had made the transition better. His thoughts were whirling. He had very little idea of who he wanted to be anymore.

It felt like a lifetime ago that Luca had stood on the platform. The decent to the Maglev station was quicker than he expected. A single Maglev car stopped at the platform.

His heart beat faster as he wondered if this could take him back to his life Outside.

The door slid back and Crisp entered.

Luca hated him. He detested his calm and unconcerned manner. He loathed his servitude to Tropolis and acceptance of his higher ranking. But most of all he despised him since his loyalty was not with his own people, that he was doing all that the Tropolite authorities wanted him to do. Crisp was little more than a traitor.

The contestants entered the car and jostled for seats followed by the guards.

Luca no longer wanted to be part of this but had no option but continue in his self-imposed imprisonment.

The door slid shut.

Luca was trapped.

Crisp stood, with drooping shoulders, glaring as he looked around the car, catching Luca's hate-filled stare.

Luca looked away. He could feel his cheeks burning as he slumped in the seat next to Eban. Crisp had appeared defeated for that one brief moment. Luca slowly rubbed his eyes with the tips of his fingers. Did he really understand the situation at all?

Crisp began his instructions. 'The Maglev will take you to the assault course ground where your progress will be transmitted live over the network.' Had Luca not seen that glimpse of sorrow, he would not have believed it. He peered up to see that Crisp was looking directly at him. 'I suggest that you spend this time to prepare mentally for the test.'

The warm glow from the car's flickering lights did nothing to calm Luca. He tried to focus his mind on the skills he had learnt, but instead the image of the notebook and the only escape took his attention. He had not told his revelation to Eban or Mercy. He glanced at them, what if he never had the chance?

No one spoke. Luca wished the metallic voice would announce something, anything to the people in the carriage, but even that failed to distract him. It seemed, on the one occasion it could have been of some use, to be switched off.

Sitting opposite Luca, Mercy frowned and questioned him with a look. Luca shook his head, dismissing her worries. He had to get through this test, survive the lower rankings and tell his friends the way out.

The dark tunnel quickly transformed into the blurred cityscape. The route was evidently not the one they had taken to come into Tropolis. It was difficult to focus on anything outside, as everything rushed past too close to the window. Luca turned away as his stomach began to churn.

After a short while, unobscured sunlight streamed into the car. The Maglev sped through open, golden space on both sides.

Luca's heart began to race once more as they headed further away from the city and into another unknown.

Eventually the Maglev began to slow and Crisp moved towards the door. The car stopped smoothly and the door slid around the carriage.

Crisp stepped out and the guards directed the contestants to follow. The gravel chips on the ground were uncomfortable to stand on with only thin rubber shoes.

The platform was surrounded with mesh fencing and topped barbed wire. Tall plants covered in greenery clung to the barriers and contained the contestants. Luca had never seen so much vegetation in one place. He smiled a little. The air had a familiar saltiness to it.

Luca absently turned and looked down the rail to see some of the tall city buildings line the horizon. Tropolis lay in a basin within the landscape. He tried to make out where Outside was but failed. Between his old life and his current situation, stood a distant city and a patchwork of fields with rough hedges, rising to the place where he now stood.

A sudden flurry of cold wind pulled at Luca's short hair. The bright day was turning. Luca breathed deeply and lifted his face to the sky. He had not felt the fresh breeze for days.

Crisp scanned his wrist at the metal security gate. There was a gentle click and a disused squeal as the door was pushed open onto a narrow dirt track. Rough low hedges lined both sides. Luca stared in awe at the strong tall plants, clumped together a short distance away. Each was much taller than a man. The tops swayed in the wind.

'You first,' instructed Crisp to one of the guards.

The guard started out, pushing aside overgrown branches. One by one the contestants followed in silent anticipation. Crisp closed the gate behind them.

Luca found himself in the centre of the group, far enough from Thickset at the front and Crisp at the rear. He shoved the branch in his way aside and flinched. The angry curved spikes which punctuated stem, stabbed his hand and scratched at his arm. He stopped and pulled the head of a thorn out of his finger. A drop of blood began to pool at the site. Luca instinctively put his finger to his mouth and sucked at it. As he turned to warn Mercy, he saw Crisp reach out to the dark shiny clusters of berries, pick one and eat it. As he did so, the harshness of his crisp features softened for just a moment. Luca was astonished that such a small thing could change a person, so he copied.

The soft fruit burst in his mouth in a mixture of juice, flesh and sweet crunchy seeds. He had never tasted anything like it before. The food in the city of Tropolis was good but this was delicious and uncomplicated. It reminded him of his own small garden and his father Outside. He reached for another, refusing to forget where he came from.

The path began to widen as they approached the top of the incline, and the vast horizon opened before them. Solitary, stunted plants grew in various spots, bent double as if constantly subjected to a fierce wind. The grey clouds were thick over the dark sea and the gentle patter of rain began to sprinkle Luca's arms with cool pinpricks. Seagulls called overhead as they drifted further inland.

A thin line of wire stretched between stakes a short distance back from the cliff edge. There was a small gap just ahead.

The group came to a silent halt.

Thickset peered over at Luca and sneered.

There was nowhere to go. They had been led up the path to the cliff edge. Luca swallowed hard as the thought struck him; the cliff edge was part of the test.

Crisp pulled his communicator out of his jacket, looked at the screen and tapped it. He remained silent despite the questioning faces. No doubt, Luca thought, enjoying his power trip.

Luca shivered as the rain cooled his skin and began to chill him. The cold wind was starting to gust stronger too.

A whirring noise overhead made him look up. A small black disc with six arms hovered above them. In the centre was a red blinking light and a small camera.

'Tropolis is ready,' Crisp announced. 'Contestants, the rules are as follows. Only ten of you will be taken to the next round. You are to complete the Endurance test by reaching the finishing line in any way you choose. Every move will be captured for the Network via mobile drones similar to the one above and other cameras on the course. Make your way to the starting line. At the sound of the alarm you may begin.' Crisp pointed to the gap in the wire fence.

Luca turned to Eban. 'He says it like we have a choice,' he whispered.

'The choice we have is to do this together,' Eban said smiling confidently.

Thickset had not been the first forward. Luca had hoped this was a good thing until his voice rose above the noise of the wind and drone. 'Terrified yet worm? You could just sit out and let the real contenders compete.'

Mercy reached out and touched Luca's arm. 'Don't rise to it. Concentrate on the task.'

The gap was narrow and the contestants had to file through one by one. The edge of the cliff was not yet dangerously close, but Luca could feel his balance toppling towards the fall.

As Luca approached the rocky edge, the beginnings of a hidden path dipped into view. The rain was falling steadily and the clouds piled up, threatening any clam that Luca could muster.

The alarm sounded.

Danita, who had sided with Thickset in the communal lounge was first to the path. Her bushy hair was blowing into her face. She was followed closely by Kit, the boy Mercy had first helped in the training room. Luca pitied Kit and his choice to be among the crowd that favoured Thickset. Maxim and Thickset ran after them confidently. Taja, the dark skinned girl, was close behind, looking determined.

Eban raced after them. 'Come on!' he called. Mercy went with him.

Luca could barely breathe as he stepped closer to the line of the cliff face. He forced himself down to the path, pressing his back up to the wall of rock as the route sloped downwards. There was no barrier and the edge dropped away into the crashing sea far below. A few hardy plants clung desperately to the rock.

Luca carefully shuffled further, shifting the loose stones under his slippery feet. Clarisse hobbled past him, precariously close to the rim of the path and disappeared around the bend. Luca shook his head and lifted his back away from the wall behind him. He placed his hand firmly against the cliff face, took a deep breath and walked along the path.

'That's it Luca!' Mercy encouraged.

As he rounded the bend, a large wooden platform had been set up in the crevice of the cliff face. It creaked under foot. Eban was sorting through an old wooden box.

'Here, take this!' He handed Luca a slightly frayed rope with a rusted clamp attached to the end. 'There are enough for everyone, but the better ones have already gone,' Eban answered Luca's glare. 'Mercy, here's one for you.' Eban passed another rope to Mercy and began to tie his own rope around his middle.

Luca copied hoping that the knot would hold. 'Pass me another one,' he said.

Mercy looked up and frowned. 'Luca, what about the others?'

Luca tried to ignore the nagging guilty sensation and looked about to find the next path leading from the platform.

A scream made him look up and the heavy rain splashed into his face. Clarisse was clinging to a long climbing rope attached to another wooden structure high above them. But above her, already on the platform, were Maxim and Thickset. They were laying down and leaning over the edge of the platform, each with a hand on Clarisse's rope and swinging the slender girl dangerously. Two other climbing ropes hung down either side of hers.

Luca hated Thickset more than ever. Mercy reached up to hold the lowest end of Clarisse's rope to steady it while Eban and Luca climbed either side of Clarisse. Not even aware of the height anymore, Luca naturally took the stance he had learned from Eban in the training room and was very soon at the same level as Clarisse. He reached out and steadied the shaking rope above her. Her screaming stopped as she thankfully sighed.

Thickset smiled cruelly as he released Clarisse and moved over to Luca's rope. Maxim grabbed onto Eban's rope.

Luca clung on to the rope as it shook and swayed. Mocking threats and laughter drifted down to him on the wind. But after a few moments it was still again.

'You can come up now,' Clarisse called.

Luca griped the wet rope and began to climb again. When he got to the platform, Clarisse was gone. He hauled himself onto the wooden boards. He dashed over to Eban's rope and helped to pull him onto the platform. Eban shook his dripping dark hair.

Luca's rope creaked and in less than a minute, Mercy had clambered up.

The rain pattered heavily on the platform leaving the green wood glistening. The wind drove the droplets hard against his skin. Luca could taste the salty sea spray mixed with in the driving rain. His t-shirt clung uncomfortably to his body and his teeth chattered.

'We need to keep moving,' he suggested.

Mercy strode to the other side of the platform. 'I don't think you are going to like this,' she called.

Luca looked on in fear. A narrow walkway continued ahead.

'But there is a rope handle,' Luca said. He was determined to be positive. He had to keep going, there were no other options. 'Look, if I loop this end of the rope round it I should be alright.'

'That wasn't what I was referring to.' Mercy pointed a little further on.

The cliff continued to rise ahead of them, and the walkway, clinging unconvincingly to the rock face, disappeared around the distant bend. A deep gash cut through the path, breaking the continuous gripping line. A river poured over the side of the land and through the gap in a torrent.

Luca gripped his rope, stepped from the platform and began towards the falls. He had to twist his arm round the rope handle before carefully re-threading his own safety rope every time the handle was attached to the rock.

Several holes had been made in the walkway where the wooden boards had snapped and smashed apart. Seeing how thin the planks were, and how easily they could fall away at any moment made Luca cringe. He looked up each time he approached a hole he would have to jump across, hoping that another boulder would not fall from above in the storm.

He could see contestants ahead of him and a few behind. If they kept his position they should go through to Intelligence since the last in his group would be ninth position.

The thundering of the falls, over the sound of the wind, announced the gash before the friends had reached it.

Luca's legs began to shake when he saw the way to cross. The balance beam that stretched from one side to the other was set slightly in front of the cascade. The steel was strong and firmly anchored at this end, but with such poor visibility, Luca had no way of knowing if the other end was tied to anything.

The wind had begun to howl and the rain fell in sheets not unlike the flowing water that had carved the gash in the cliff face.

'I can't do that,' Luca called over the roaring water and buffeting wind.

Mercy frowned. 'But we have to,' she said calmly. 'I can't believe they are making us do this.'

Eban skirted around Luca and was peering at the waterfall.

'You know what, I think there is a way behind this.' Eban leaned over the barrier that directed the contestants to the balance beam. 'Look, at that flat section. I think there is a path.'

Eban climbed over the barrier and carefully edged himself towards the falls, his back pressed against the rock face.

Luca's mouth went dry.

Eban beckoned to them.

Luca shook his head.

'Come on Luca.' Mercy pulled at his arm. 'Eban's found a better way.' She gave him a gentle nudge. 'Crisp said that we could do this anyway we liked. We don't have to do it the Tropolis way.'

The thought of rebelling against the Tropolis way, woke something inside of Luca. He lifted his face to the sky, opened his mouth and took a gulp of rain water. If this ended in disaster, he would, at least be doing it as an Outsider and not controlled by Tropolis.

'Do you want me to go first?' Mercy asked.

Luca laughed sarcastically. 'No!' He un-looped his rope and clambered over the barrier. Eban had made his way back and offered his hand.

'We'll do this together. The first bit is the worst.'

The surface was not just rain soaked but slippery with green moss. The consistent water had smoothed the rocks and the path was shallow. But, just a few metres in, a deeper path had been cut into the cliff face that was quite protected from the wind, rain and waterfall.

The sound of the crashing of the water filled his ears and saturated the place with vibrations.

There were no cameras peering down on them in this secluded space.

'I found out how to ...' Luca began, thinking it was safe. But then a drone slipped into the entrance behind the falls, following their progress, the red blinking light indicating the camera below. It swayed about recklessly in the buffeting wind, but as it neared them, the relatively still air held it steady.

Luca shook his head. 'Don't worry.' He shooed the others along.

A massive overhang of rock provided the thick ceiling of the cavern behind the falls. The roar of the water filled the space and ensured no other sound could be heard. The darkened sea was barely visible through the whooshing water and clouds of mist. Although the path led behind the falls, a section branched off to a slit in the rock to one side, wide enough for Luca to walk through. The reprise from the storm made the path eerily still.

As they neared the exit on the far side, a flash of lightning lit the sheet of water, flooding the cavern with sudden brightness. The wind whipped at the edges of the waterfall shifting the spray across the path and drenching the friends in icy water.

The rocky track on the other side was treacherous with fallen rocks. Eban took the lead once again, with Luca ahead of Mercy.

As he emerged from the shelter of the falls, Luca saw a lone dark figure walking slowly along the steel beam. Through the blurring rain he watched as the boy balanced uneasily at the shock of seeing the group. He took a step forward, rushing to get to the end of the beam before Luca could re-join the route. His arms began to flail and his body swayed. He twisted in an attempt to regain his balance. Then, as if the wind had shoved him, the boy's toes slipped and he lost his footing, his body rolled backwards and he tumbled down in the cascade of rain. His scream was swallowed up with the thunder of the falls.

Luca did not even know his name.

Mercy pushed past Luca, screaming, and ran to the barrier.

Eban and Luca held her back.

'Why are they doing this?' she sobbed.

Eban shook his head and pulled Mercy into a hug.

'We need to get away from this place,' Luca said as he dared to look down. The waves and torrent from the waterfall swelled below in a mix of froth and foam. The dark water crashed against the cliff face but there was no body. 'What if others have got past us?'

At the far side, a thick scramble net swayed in the wind. Water sprayed from the thrashing cords as it hit against the sheer rock. Mercy climbed quietly, flanked by Eban and Luca. The rough rope was cold in Luca's hands, but he was grateful for it; he needed to know that this was reality or he would just give up now and wait for the nightmare to finish.

Another long and winding wooden walkway clung to the cliff, which continued to rise higher above them as if it was growing out of the sea and trying to reach into the dark sky. The sodden planks dipped a little with each step, threatening to give way under their weight. Luca was grateful for the rope handle that continued beside the steep path. He continued to loop his own rope around it but also used it to drag himself up the cliff face and further away from the crashing waves.

Another flash of lightning briefly lit the grey rain filled sky before a blindingly bright bolt cut through the air and forked into the sea. There was a moment of almost silence before the bang and rippling of thunder completely filled the space. Luca's whole body could feel the vibrations that only seemed amplified by the solid rock beside him.

It was barely over before another strike shot across the sky and the thunder bellowed.

The beating rain and wind continued to get stronger.

Mercy's teeth chattered and Luca could see that her skin was becoming pale.

'We need to move faster,' Luca urged loudly.

Eban laughed but his smile soon vanished when he turned and saw Mercy. He urged them forward at a quicker pace. He rounded the bend then shuffled back quickly. Luca grabbed Mercy's arm as she slipped. Something zoomed past.

'Hey!' Luca shouted.

Eban quickly helped Luca pull Mercy to the rock face.

'Ambush!' Eban announced his brows furrowed. 'How are we going to get through?'

Luca shook his head not understanding Eban.

'Thickset and his mates are shooting,' Eban explained.

'What?' Luca shuffled past Mercy and Eban. 'Keep her safe.' Eban nodded.

He gripped his rope tightly and slowly rounded the bend. The boards were slick with blood. The motionless body of Clarisse blocked the path, her own saturated blonde hair plastered over her face. An arrow remained in her chest and a gunshot wound in her leg. Luca gagged.

Propped up against the wall, next to Clarisse, a silver haired girl had an arrow in her side. Luca thought that he could make out her breathing. The path was blocked with the girls' bodies but ended with a platform with no further route from it. It sat within a natural horseshoe cove of the cliff. A glimmering metal hook and a short rope hung from the opposite cliff face.

Thickset and Maxim stood on the platform, armed with a crossbow and a small black gun. They were laughing although Luca couldn't hear them. They were facing some targets that were set up at a distance, maybe the length of the shooting range in the training rooms. They aimed and fired. Thickset's arrow never made it through the storm but Maxim had managed to hit the outer marks on the target. Thickset threw the crossbow to one side in frustration. It slid over the planks, began to tip, then fell out of sight and into the sea. He snatched the gun from Maxim who had been laughing even more and then fired again at the target. The bull's eye emitted a puff of smoke. Above Thickset's head, a shining metal harpoon with rope attached, exploded from the rock and fired across the gap, embedding in the cliff face on the other side. Thickset ducked and turned at the sudden movement. He saw Luca and raised the gun. Luca sped around the bend. The loud bang and the shattering of rock at the corner, just short of Luca's head made him catch his breath.

He crouched low and peered around the corner. Thickset fired again.

'Stay back,' Eban shouted.

Lightning lit the sea as another bolt made contact with the water. Thunder cracked and the wooden boards shook.

Luca waited, but Thickset never appeared at the corner.

Luca dared to look again. Thickset was on the other side of the cove, beckoning to Maxim who had looped his rope over the suspended line. Maxim screamed as he launched himself from the platform. His momentum carried him to the far side where Thickset grabbed his leg and pulled him to the cliff face. He dropped heavily to the walkway below. Thickset lifted the gun and aimed at the rope. The bang echoed in the cove. Again he aimed, but no noise followed. Thickset grimaced, pounded the gun against the wall and then threw it away with disgust. He stared up at Luca and then sped along the path, vanishing into the storm.

'Come on,' Luca encouraged, 'they're gone.'

He stepped over the injured girl and Clarisse, trying not to think of what they were. The rain was quickly diluting and washing away the remnants of blood from the boards.

He reached up and tested the suspended rope. It gave a little but seemed secure. There was nothing left to hit the targets with except maybe rocks, but to throw that far and that accurately could take too long. Mercy, pale with cold, knelt beside the silver haired girl.

They had to use the rope line that had already been set up.

'Penny?' Mercy said as she placed her fingers to the girl's neck. 'Help me with her,' she called. 'She's still alive.'

'We don't have time,' Luca protested rushing back towards them. 'We need to keep moving. Others may have got past us when we were behind the waterfall.'

'Luca,' Eban said frowning at him. 'We can't leave her here. What's wrong with you?'

'How are you going to get her across that?' Luca pointed to the rope. 'The others used it as a kind of slide. You can't carry her over that.'

'How did they do it?' Eban asked.

'Tied their rope over the top.'

Eban leaned over Clarisse and carefully untied her rope. 'Using this and Penny's we have two. We can get her across. One of us can catch her at the other end.'

Luca shrugged his shoulders and puffed. 'Whatever. Let's get moving.'

Eban helped to create a sling that held Penny under the arms before he took the ride to the other side first. Luca lifted Penny. Her eyes flickered and then shut once again. All of a sudden, Luca's shame doubled. He had intended to leave her there. Mercy remained silent as she arranged the ropes and secured Penny.

'Ready?' she called.

Luca waved to Eban and he gave the thumbs up. They launched Penny over the gap. She sped over the open water. Eban clambered up the rock face a little, caught her and managed to release her, not without effort and tugging. Luca was ready to send Mercy after her and help, but Mercy waited patiently much to Luca's annoyance.

Mercy had a fraction of colour back in her cheeks when she kicked off the side. The exertion had obviously warmed her a little. Eban caught her confidently. Mercy jumped down and immediately crouched over Penny.

Luca had come a long way in his understanding of friendship. He knew that Eban would catch him before he hit the wall. Luca tried not to think about what he was doing. The rain splashed into his eyes as he looped his rope over the line. He tugged on the rope. Eban waved his arms and shouted something but his voice was lost in the hammering rain and blasting wind.

Luca twisted his hands into the rope and allowed himself to slip down the line. The rope quickly cut into his wrists but as he was almost halfway across, he could endure it a moment longer.

The line suddenly jerked and then slackened as it snapped. Luca's rope came free from the broken line. Luca yelled as he fell towards the pounding waves.

Chapter 19

Luca's mouth filled with water as the sea welcomed him into her deathly embrace.

The swirling water tossed him and tugged at his fragile body. He thrashed his legs and stretched up his arms in the hope that he was heading for the surface. The bubbles and foaming water broke over his face and suddenly he was able to fill his lungs with air.

The vast, dark cliff face filled his view. He twisted in the water only to be bombarded by a high wave. Water filled his ears, and he coughed as he came back to the surface.

Luca had seen the waves crashing into the rock wall since this task had begun, and although the safety of the cliff face was appealing he knew he had to move away before he was broken by the force of the water on the sharp shards.

He gulped in some air and began to swim against the incoming swell.

His leg muscles burned and the water dragged through his t-shirt. But he still swam.

Another wave broke over him. But he was not defeated.

The effort to push forward as he rose before the crest of the wave, left him panting. But he would not give in to the sea.

As the wave broke beyond him, Luca knew that he had made a brave escape but it was not over. He continued to attack the oncoming waves and made his way out of the cove. He should never to let himself be trapped by the power of the crest that would carry him back towards the rock face. Luca kept a safe distance from the cliffs.

Out of the shelter of cove and the swirling water there, he floated on the undulating waves. Luca saw the vast sea. He rested for a moment and looked back.

The rocky cliffs rose high above him. The wooden walkway, clinging to the face was just about discernible, yet there was no sign of Mercy and Eban. Luca scanned the walkway, blinking the salt water and rain out of his eyes. He followed the line of the thin planks hugging the stone as it descended to a beach some distance away.

Luca's heart was racing and his muscles were already burning. The thought of having to swim that far almost defeated him. He looked about hopelessly for some kind of float. Nothing.

A bubble of air popped out from the neck of his t-shirt and caught his attention.

He struggled to take off his soaking t-shirt and leaned back in the water to rest a little. Luca, untangled the fabric and tied a firm knot in the large opening. His head went below the surface of the water as he worked. Luca pounded the sea with his hands, came back up and spat out the salty water. With his feet pummelling the water below, he opened the t-shirt up as much as possible and allowed the wind to fill it with air. Snatching the neck and arm holes shut, he held it close to his chest. The air filled sack lifted him higher in the water. Luca sighed.

As he allowed the t-shirt float to take his weight, tiny bubbles fizzed through the fabric.

Luca shivered.

With the t-shirt held tightly, and the cliff face a safe distance to his right side, Luca floated on his back and kicked his weary legs pushing him closer to the beach. The rain prickled his face.

Every few minutes, Luca checked his position. He was relieved to see the beach getting closer. He opened the t-shirt above the waves and re-filled it with air before snatching the fabric shut again.

A bolt of lightning touched down on the cliff top not too far away, bathing the scene in stark white.

The water currents were changing, and Luca could feel the tug of the tide pulling him in the right direction. He breathed deeply, knowing he was nearly there. The waves began to carry him towards the beach. He flipped over onto his stomach, teeth chattering, and tested for the sea bed under his feet, finding pebbles and sand that shifted under him. He tucked his shaking legs underneath him and stood in the shallow water. His arms hung heavily at his sides, one hand still clutching the sagging t-shirt float. His legs felt like lead weights. The waves still came rushing in and he braced himself against their repeated efforts to knock him down. He teetered towards the shoreline

He turned as his name was carried on the wind.

At the foot of the cliff a small crowd of people in multi-coloured shirts were stood together. A fiery orange-clad person was rushing towards him.

'Luca!' Eban shouted as he dashed to his side and flung a soft white towel over Luca's shoulders.

Eban lifted Luca's arm over his own shoulder then held Luca's waist. Eban half lifted, half guided him up the beach. The pebbles slipped and clattered under foot.

'You are amazing!' Eban laughed. 'We saw you swimming out to sea and then disappear. We are so glad you made it.'

'I'm too late,' Luca muttered through his shaking.

'No,' Eban said. 'Not too late!' Then his tone changed to one of sadness. 'Clarisse was killed, the other lad on the beam didn't make it either and Walden, the only one left behind us had no way of getting across the gap with the rope broken.'

'I'm through?'

'The others thought you were gone. But Mercy and I knew you'd make it.'

'Penny?' Luca asked.

'She's alright. The arrow didn't do any major damage. They were waiting for her when we got to the finishing place on the beach.'

'Poor Clarisse.'

'I know.' Eban let Luca take more of his own weight as they approached the group.

Crisp appeared almost amused by Luca's arrival.

'This way,' he announced, rain water dripping from his hair.

'Don't we need to wait for Walden and for someone to fetch Clarisse?'

Crisp turned. 'No,' he replied bluntly.

He led the tired contestants over the high pebble bank and along a concrete path. Luca dragged his feet and snuggled into the dry towel.

Lightning flashed through the clouds above but the thunder took longer to start to rumble. The storm was moving on.

A Maglev waited, warm and dry, at the platform as if nothing extraordinary happened.

Chapter 20

The latch clicked and the door opened. With effort, Luca removed his wrist from the scanner. Every movement was laboured. The light automatically switched on as he entered his room as the day, still not finished, was dull and overcast.

Luca was exhausted, but the raucous laughter coming from the seating area left him on edge.

'I'll grab my stuff,' Eban said and he looked nervously towards Thickset tucking into a large plate of food.

Mercy hadn't spoken a word since the test.

'I think she needs to be kept safe,' Luca whispered to Eban and then turned to Mercy. 'Where do you want to be?' he asked her gently.

'I'll be round in a little while,' she replied. 'Your room feels most like home here.' She smiled sadly.

Luca could feel the last sustaining wall breaking inside of him. He quickly shut the door behind him and slumped to the floor.

This place could never be home. It should never be home.

Home was a place of make believe, found only in the pages of a book once read to him by a mother he sorely missed. He existed only in a place of fear, poverty and imprisonment.

He tipped his head back to the wall and closed his eyes. The memory of Clarisse's motionless, blood-soaked body flashed inside his mind. There was no escape from death.

The pounding waves still echoed in his mind and he desperately wanted to flee from the torment that was aimed right at his heart. He understood, partially, what it could have been like to nearly drown. He had now experienced what his mother had endured in her last moments. Willow had not been forced like he had, by means of a cruel competition, but she had nonetheless been pushed to the limit by Tropolis. She had struggled to take care of Luca and his father, she had no chance in the waters at the dock. She had as little value as Luca, in the eyes of Tropolis. For many years he had believed that perhaps there was no way to save his mother, but after what he had witnessed today, he knew otherwise. No one had helped her. Luca was certain that the Tropolis ships had life belts and ropes but they had chosen not to use them. Tropolis only cared for itself. Today, it couldn't even be bothered to collect the wasted bodies.

Death had been so close yet had spared him this time, but he had felt its sting. He had seen the results left by the inevitable force. One was the moment of an accident, yet he was partly to blame. The other was an act of will, a murder worthy of Tropolis. He had escaped, but for how long?

Hot tears flooded his eyes, but Luca was not sure if they were for sorrow, anger or fear. In his exhaustion of body and spirit, curled up on the floor.

A while later someone knocked at the door.

Luca wiped his face with the soft white towel, scanned his wrist and let Eban in.

'You look a mess.' Eban said as he put an arm round Luca's shoulder and guided him to the bathroom. Luca took a stuttering breath.

Eban fetched a pile of dry clothes. 'Take a shower and wash all that dirt away. You shouldn't have to carry that anymore. You can't change what has happened.'

Luca looked at Eban in surprise.

'If we can't change anything,' Luca replied weakly, 'I don't know what we are doing here.'

Eban turned the dial on the shower and a burst of hot water and steam poured out. 'I never said we can't change anything. But what is done is now gone. You need to stop looking back at it. Things that are happening now and next, will always have something within your power to change.'

Eban hummed a little and shut the door behind him leaving Luca alone in the warm bathroom.

Something he could change? There was nothing in this competition that he could change. But what if he was no longer in the hands of Tropolis? He had found out a way to escape in the lifetime before the Endurance test. He would leave Tropolis and take his friends with him. At last he had found something of value in this diseased place. He had found true companionship. Mercy and Eban had from the very start of their journey to Tropolis been the ones to rally round him, to build him up, to show him his strengths. Now he could do something for them, and give them back what he owed. He could bring relief to Mercy's suffering.

Luca let the hot soapy water remove the salty crust from his skin and hair. It even relieved his aching muscles a little. He walked out of the bathroom in his dry clothes .

'Better?' Eban asked when Luca walked into the room in his clean dry clothes.

'Kind of.' Luca stretched out on the sofa.

Eban patted him on the shoulder.

Luca stretched out on the sofa and looked up at the blinking red light of the camera, and picked up his tablet. 'Suppose we should study.'

'Don't you want to eat first?'

Luca nodded, dragged himself up from the sofa and peered out of his room. The lounge was empty but the smell of warm bread and spices filled the air. He ladled the thick soup into a deep bowl, grabbed a couple of rolls and a large slice of chocolate cake. He walked back to his room and handed the tray to Eban.

'Take these.' Luca scanned his wrist and his door opened. 'I'm going to get Mercy.'

The stillness was only ruined by the flashing red lights from the cameras. Luca scowled.

He tapped gently at Mercy's door. He could hear movement but there was no answer. He waited and knocked again.

'Mercy? It's Luca.'

The door clicked and opened.

She had changed back into white trousers and a chunky jumper. Her dark hair was wet but combed. But her eyes were swollen and blotchy.

'Are you alright?' Luca asked.

'I will be.' Mercy tried to smile a little, but her face was still full of sadness.

'Are you still coming to work?'

Mercy padded out with bare feet and the door swung shut behind her. 'Of course. I'll just grab something to eat.'

Luca waited, holding his own door open for her. He watched as she took a small plate and approached the table. She did not hurry, despite only taking some warm, buttered rolls and a small bunch of grapes.

Eban was sat on the floor at the coffee table when they joined him. He had already eaten half the pie and was mashing up the potatoes in the gravy. Mercy perched on the soft chair with her small plate, while Luca slowly lowered himself to the floor.

The steam lifted lazily from the soup in misty swirls. The aroma was rich and had hints of familiarity. His first mouthful was hot and comforting, almost as if he could have prepared it on one of those rare days when one of his own plants had produced its harvest. Luca could feel the difference the hopeful food produced.

With a stomach full, Luca began to feel sleepy. He knew he needed to tell the others what he had discovered and he couldn't wait for lights out. He picked up the tablet from the sofa.

'We need to talk.'

Eban smiled and nodded.

'No, follow me.'

Luca strolled into the bathroom and the others followed. He closed the door on the camera that surveyed his room.

Luca perched on the side of the bath and motioned for the others to draw close.

'I've worked out how the others got out of Tropolis,' Luca began in a whisper. 'You know, all those missing people, the ones they say are dead. The answer was right there in front of us. The rubbish chute. In the notebook. It said it in the notebook.'

Eban's eyes widened. 'Out with the rubbish. That could work.'

'We can't stay here. We have to leave,' Luca continued. He picked up his tablet. 'Do you think Tropolis have plans of this building somewhere on the Network.'

'They may.' Eban said shrugging.

Luca tapped the screen and it lit up. He stared.

'What is it?' Mercy asked leaning in closer. She gasped.

Eban looked down at the tablet.

Suddenly the bathroom door lock clicked and the door sprung open. There was no one there, the room was empty. Luca tugged at the door but it would not shut again, as it was now fixed in place. The flashing red light of the camera from the main room seemed more intense. Tropolis did not like to be kept out of the conversation.

The three friends returned to the sofa exchanging glances but refusing to say a word.

Luca held the tablet close to him.

They had all seen it before it had faded away.

The home screen was now safely back in view. But moments before, the screen showed an image of a flower with five heart shaped petals. The flower from the notebook. The flower tattooed on Mercy's neck that Luca had noticed and they had discussed so long ago.

The on-screen image had been displayed with a caption.

BE READY

Chapter 21

There would be no lights out.

Luca knew that they would be watched all night.

'We could try one of your rooms,' Luca suggested.

Mercy shook her head. 'The cameras are everywhere,' she said. 'Wherever we go, they will watch us,' Luca knew it to be true. He thought, that maybe, they would even be kept apart if they tried since it appeared they could and would control the doors.

Luca could not concentrate on studying for the Intelligence Test. His mind was busy with unanswered questions. Who would leave a message, and why give it to him? How had it got there? Did they know about the notebook? Luca had carefully and secretly checked that it still remained in his pocket. He was grateful that no one had removed the used clothes and discovered it in his trousers while they were risking their lives in the Endurance Test, but that did not mean that no one had seen it.

Luca curled up in the chair pretending to sleep. He worried about the next test. Each time his chances of surviving were getting smaller, the chances for all of them were smaller. He could not look at Eban or Mercy.

When he was on the Outside, he had known it was not wise to form friendships. They were rare and now he fully understood why. He had thought that having a friend would be another way to be disappointed and let down. They would inevitably take the best gleans and steal credits. Working with another Outsider would reduce your likelihood of finding what you needed to live another day. Luca had often considered why any Outsider would ever find a partner and have children, as surely it would make them weaker. He had never really understood until now.

Having a friend meant losing them one day.

Luca shifted a little in the chair, hiding his face in the cushions.

If you had no friends it could not hurt. His grief was already a heavy burden. It was one that he had carried for such a long time. He did not want to add to it.

He regretted ever making friends.

Luca finally drifted off to sleep, weary from the Endurance test, feeling lonely and sad that he could not share his load.

The next morning began with a beautifying session. Franco could not contain his excitement.

'I thought you were gone when I watched. I almost died!' Franco began, gripping Luca's shoulders and staring at his reflection. Luca clenched his fists; he had almost died. 'What an amazing show! Loved the danger, loved the storm, loved the shooting! What a great way to build on last year. So glad that the Network is finally listening to what we want.'

Luca sat motionless. What was this man saying? He had not understood at all. Endurance was a horrendous test that had no value and no place in a humane society. Luca could not recognise the man before him.

'You were incredible!' Franco continued to flow. 'And I think that Tropolis are going to love you today. You have shot up the rating within my sector. The beautifiers are quite jealous that you are mine! Nothing was going to stop you. Unlike that girl that dropped you into the sea in the first place.' Luca frowned. 'Well,' Franco continued, seeing Luca's confusion. 'If she had just left that other girl alone, like you did, you would have been safe. But then I guess there wouldn't have been the drama.'

Luca looked down. He no longer wanted to see his own face. Franco was right, if it had been up to him he would have left Penny where she was. She would have died just like Clarisse. Only it would not have been Thickset who had given the fatal blow. What had he become? He was popular in Tropolis. It made him feel sick.

Franco still wasn't finished. 'I don't know why you helped them at all. You could have got higher up the ratings and saved my poor little heart from fretting!' Franco said patting his chest. 'You know how to make me worry.' He returned to his workstation as if he had said nothing out of the ordinary, and began to mix some cream.

Someone grabbed Luca's hand. He looked up only to be greeted by the red belted lady and a pin prick on the end of his finger. She no longer smiled or even spoke to the competitors. He snatched his hand away. She sniffed and inserted the card into the slot.

Luca scratched his nose as he tried to understand. Franco obviously thought that Luca was helping Eban and Mercy, but in fact it had been the other way round.

'They're good people, Franco.' Luca said as he thought about them. They were kind and helpful. If they had not befriended him, he would have been dead a long time ago. 'And besides, I don't think I'd be here now without them.'

'Don't be over dramatic,' Franco said lifting his hand as if to say stop. 'You don't need them.' He started to smear the concoction on Luca's arms. 'Anyway,' Franco continued as he rubbed in the cream. 'I don't know why she even bothered. I mean, just look at the one she took across that zip wire before you.'

Luca turned and saw Penny's pale reflection. He had been surprised to see her in the lift, as he had expected her to be out of the competition.

'I don't even know how she is here,' Luca mused.

'They fixed her. Apparently it was a simple procedure. If I know Decipio, her beautifier, he would have arranged for some extra help. I would not trust him. She should not be left in this contest at all.' Franco lowered his voice. 'If I gave advice, which of course I'm not allowed to give out, I would say you need to be more ruthless. Do you want to win this or not? Stop letting others push you around. Tropolis want to love you, and you can't win unless they do. I think you have what it takes.'

If leaving people to die on a cliff ledge was what it takes to win, both he and Thickset would be in the final.

'Another big day today,' Franco continued. 'Intelligence is one of my favourites. I wonder what twist it will have this time.'

'So the tests are same for each competition?'

'Mostly,' Franco said now rubbing a clear gel over Luca's face. 'They have the same titles but they vary. I mean, you are nearly there now. Intelligence today, then there will be the interview; that is always interesting. Then one more popularity vote as we have seen what you are all like now. So all you need to do is get through this one, then it will be simple.'

Along with the camera and crew, a large screen had already been set up in front of the sofas in the holding area. The picture had been divided into two. Half the screen showed a large score board with each of the contestants' names. They ranged from Danita, the curly haired, graceful and strong girl who came first in the Endurance test, to Kit, the short boy that Mercy had helped the first time they had entered the training room. He had managed to avoid leaving the competition by beating them to the start line.

Luca watched Kit as he wearily walked away from his beautifier to the holding area. There were no indications of the turmoil that had occurred the previous day. All external signs had been eradicated completely; the soul, however, was much harder to heal.

Luca did his best to steady his nerves as he fixed his gaze once again on the screen. Next to the scoreboard section, the other half of the screen showed the image of two white chairs and very little else.

The contestants sat quietly. No one needed to stand anymore. Thickset still spread himself out, but Luca could see he was anxious too by his lack of smile.

A few moments later the announcer came over the speaker and the first two contestants were called forward. Thickset and Maxim, the one that had been with Thickset when Clarisse was shot, were led by a guard through an almost invisible white door to the side of the holding area. Almost immediately, they appeared on the screen but there was no sound being transmitted.

They sat down. Luca concluded that the chairs must have been fairly large as both contestants who were both tall and muscular looked more child-like when sat in them. Next, they leaned forward and wrapped a piece of fabric around each ankle. Then they settled back.

After a short while Maxim briefly flinched in his chair and opened his mouth while Thickset first smirked then looked fiercely determined. Luca could hear muffled shouts from the room. Time and time again, each of the contestants jerked but Luca thought Thickset came away with less incidents.

When finally the strange and horrific test had finished, Thickset and Maxim staggered out of the room and slumped onto the sofas.

Despite the macabre show, it was difficult not to watch. Luca knew that he would be called soon. He was both angered and intrigued to know what was happening in what was meant to be an intelligence test.

After Thickset and Maxim, Danita was set against Taja. Luca was certain that this would be a fairly level match yet Danita proved more resolute than Taja.

Kit and Eban were called into the room next. Kit hardly flinched at all while Eban still smiled despite the intermittent jumps. The only times when the Eban sat still and Kit twitched was when Kit had spoken with evidently a wrong reply of some kind.

Luca bit down on his lip. There were only four contestants yet to be called. He fixed his eyes on the screen trying not to think about what he would do if he was put against Mercy.

Eban appeared peaceful, even when he twitched in his seat. Kit on the other hand had a fierce determination about him. His hands gripped at the seat tightly.

Luca's heart began to race as Eban removed the straps and left the room.

'Luca and Penny. Go to the testing room.'

Luca gave a deep sigh as he got to his feet. He would not have to decide how to play against Mercy. He could now just do his best to win.

The room was cool but had a metallic taste in the air.

Luca sat in the large chair while a voice instructed him to wrap the fabric strips around each ankle. He nervously did as instructed.

Penny looked attentive and determined. Her bright blue eyes were narrowed. She tucked a loose strand of dead straight hair behind her ear. Luca felt unsettled. Penny would not give up easily. He had seen what she had overcome in the Endurance Test.

A man's dull voice filled the room. Luca was used to the Tropolite way of communicating, but still looked for the man himself. High in the wall, the line of windows showed the panel of judges sitting in the vantage place of another space. They were not paying attention to Luca or Penny but were in deep conversation with each other, except for the man on the end. He appeared weary with the task ahead.

Luca watched as the man's lips moved and the message was broadcast to the testing room.

'During the Intelligence test you will be asked a series of questions based on the information that you have been given to study. The questions that you will be asked are the same as all the other contestants. Your reaction time and correct answers will determine where you emerge on the score board. Questions will begin in ten seconds.'

Luca's hands went cold. He could hear his speeding breaths roaring in the silent room. He peered up at the protected gallery room. A large screen counted down the seconds.

'Who is the founder of the Tropolis Establishment Ruling?' Luca jumped at the sound of the voice.

'Harland Barret,' answered Penny quickly, far too quickly for Luca.

A sharp pain ran through the soles of Luca's feet and his body jerked under the rippling vibrations of the power charge. It stopped as suddenly as it started. Luca let out a gasp as he realised this was the result of a not being the first to answer. He looked up the judges and noticed the screen flashing up the next question. He read it then looked over at Penny. She was just like so many other Outsiders; she had never been taught how to read.

'What does the Tropolis Establishment Ruling protect?' the man read clearly.

Luca looked back at the screen and read out the answer. 'The people and land of Tropolis.'

Penny twitched in her seat. Luca felt a twist in his stomach but he refused to acknowledge it.

'How many amendments have been made to the Tropolis Establishment Ruling?'

'Twelve,' answered Luca quickly.

Penny let out a squeal.

'The last amendment states that 'Tropolis will continue to uphold' what?'

Luca couldn't recall the answer. He glanced at Penny who had screwed up her eyes and was tapping her head. He knew the answer would be on the screen. He leaned back, to appear that he was trying to think, peered at the screen, looked back at the ground then answered. 'The rights of the Tropolite people above and beyond the rights of all others.' He could hear his monotone cheating voice. He waited for the next question, desperately trying not to notice the sobs coming from Penny.

'Name one right you give up when you become a Tropolite citizen?' Question after question. 'What was the highest ranking scientific advancement of the last decade?' Penny was being given shock after shock. 'Who is Chief of State?' Luca was fearless in his pursuit of victory.

Luca did not understand the frown Eban gave him as he returned to the sofa or why Mercy's eyes sparkled with tears. He had completed the questions and he knew that he had given the right answers. He would not be sent to his death, at least not today.

Penny sobbed from the other side of the room, still clearly shaken by the shocks and her inevitable position on the score board. Her name would now sit at the lowest position due to Luca's choices in the Intelligence test.

Luca slumped onto the sofa and stared at the floor. What had he done? He would not be sent to the Death Room but someone else would be. His friends were disgusted with him. He let that sink in for a moment and then wished he had acted in a more honourable way.

Thickset had looked so nervous before his test but now lounged with confidence. Luca could not bring himself to do the same. Thickset had proved himself to be a better person.

He glanced up at the screen where the next contestant now sat.

Luca had not heard them call her name.

Mercy appeared even smaller in the large chair but Luca saw her quickly fit the cuff to her leg.

Opposite her sat one of Thickset's followers, an older boy with wide, brown eyes. He looked as if he could flatten Mercy. But Luca knew that Mercy had studied hard and he had left her space in the scores to slot easily above the lowest contestants.

After a few moments the first shock was given and Mercy jumped in her seat. Luca frowned.

The second shock twitched at Mercy followed by the third and fourth.

Luca shifted to the edge of his seat. What was she doing? He knew that Mercy knew the answers to the questions, he had studied with her and Eban. Why was she staying silent?

Luca looked to Mercy's contestant. He looked confused. At last Mercy would gain some points. Mercy opened her mouth and then jolted in her chair once more. Had she really given the wrong answer?

Not once did her contestant shudder.

Luca's hands began to shake and his eyes filled with tears.

Mercy silently staggered out of the testing room.

'What did you do?' demanded Luca.

Mercy did not reply.

Nolan Smythe appeared on the large screen.

'Welcome fellow Tropolites to the results of the Intelligence Test. Our contestants are patiently awaiting the results which will be with us in a few moments. In the meantime, let us have a look at some of the highlights of this year's competition.'

The speakers blasted out a loud and happy tune, but the images did not match the tone. Luca was reminded of the series of events that had led him to this moment. There was still a hint of excitement in the first scenes. He did not feel the same anymore. Sweat dripped down his back as he shifted his feet uneasily. Today the over-riding emotion was fear. He squeezed his eyes shut. He did not want to relive the events or watch Tropolis embellish it with glory.

Nolan's voice announced the video had finished and Luca dared to watch once again.

'And now for the most recent results. Who will succeed?' Nolan winked.

The screen split into ten with each contestant featuring in one of the sections.

The first question was read out and each contestant responded either with an answer or a look of pain. Points were awarded for the correct answer and the speed with which it was answered. Luca, of course, scored zero while Penny, who had answered just one question swiftly and correctly, managed three points.

Luca watched himself. He watched as the person on the screen raced off the correct answers, each time the aching in his stomach grew. He drew his arms around himself. The score grew.

He glanced at Mercy on the screen. She grimaced in pain; her score never leaving zero.

He wanted to hide.

Reliving his ugly behaviour made him want to vomit. He knew he had been wrong, but deep down, in the hideous secret part of him that looked too similar to Franco, he had thought that he had to do it to survive. He had left himself no other choice.

Nolan Smythe was still smiling when the test scores were complete.

Mercy and Penny were at the bottom of the list. Mercy's scores had progressively got worse after each test, but there was no escaping this time.

There was no noise and no voice to warn him. It was as if everything outside of himself had been silenced. All Luca could hear was the drumming of his heart and the short stuttering breaths he was making.

Everything happened in slow motion. The scene was being transmitted over the network delayed by just a few moments. Thickset was punching the air, Penny was crying and Mercy was getting to her feet.

Luca turned quickly towards Mercy.

She stood confidently, her face composed but with sorrow in her eyes.

She turned towards Eban and whispered urgently to him. She then reached over to Luca and squeezed his hand.

So many had already lost. Luca imagined all the times this cruel competition had taken place over the years. Outsiders like him, like Thickset, like Penny had entered and had been destroyed. But there had never been anyone like Mercy. She put others before herself, she extended her hand even though it meant that she fell further down the rankings. Did she know what she was doing? How could she do that to herself? How could she do that to him? He needed her.

'Mercy!' Luca moaned . 'No!' He grasped her hand with both of his. 'I'm sorry. I'm so sorry.'

The Tropolite guards approached suddenly. Luca stood and quickly positioned himself in front of Mercy. He stretched out his arms, trying to protect her.

Mercy gently put her hand on his shoulder. 'Friends forgive one another and I will always be your friend, Luca,' she whispered leaning close. She ducked under his arm and hugged him. He held onto her tightly. 'It's time to go now. It's finished,' she said quietly.

Mercy pulled herself free from his grip. There was no need for the guards to grab her and force her towards the door. She turned, took Penny's arm and went willingly to the death room.

Chapter 22

The air was too thin. Luca struggled to breathe. He pulled at clumps of his hair trying to understand what had just happened. Mercy had known the answers yet she had deliberately stayed silent.

Luca had seen the look of disappointment when he had returned to his seat. She had known that he had cheated and had taken his place, the place he had forced onto Penny.

'Calm down Luca, please.'

Luca thought he could hear someone speaking to him but everything was too overwhelming.

His head hurt.

He opened his clenched fists and saw clumps of his own russet hair.

'My fault. My fault.'

'Quietly Luca,' Eban hushed. 'Come on, calm down.'

Luca let his hands drop to his lap. 'My fault. It's all my fault.' He clamped his hand over his mouth as he realised what he was confessing.

Thickset whooped and waved franticly along with the other triumphant contestants at the camera as the red light blinked off.

Eban pulled Luca from the sofa and guided him behind the depleted group towards the lift.

'They will punish you. Watch out!' Crisp said in a hushed voice as they filed past him.

They had already punished him beyond what he thought he could handle. The crushing darkness of loss was swallowing him. A vast and growing wave rose up and threatened to drown him this time. He should let it take him. He deserved nothing better. He could not remember how he had managed to battle grief before, he had no plan and no raft to carry him on the crest. This was why he should never have let the barbed wire fence come down, this was why Outsiders never had friends. The loss was just too much to bear. The guilt was overwhelming.

Eban pulled him from the lift, scanned his wrist at the door and took him to the bed. Luca did not fight as Eban lay him down and placed the blanket over him.

'You need to rest.'

'Why did she do it?'

'She has a plan,' Eban replied sadly. 'She knew she wouldn't win the contest.'

'She should have stayed Outside then.'

'We need to trust her.'

Luca closed his eyes. He would never trust anyone again.

Not a single light shone out over the dark city. Luca had fallen asleep quickly, exhausted and desperate to get away from reality. But now, he was wide awake and aware.

The thin glass wall that separated Luca from the dramatic drop was cold under his fingertips. He felt an affinity with the darkness. For Luca, there had always been a little light somewhere within him, even when he was Outside, but now he had snuffed it out.

Eban had not stayed, and he understood why. Just his pale reflection in the glass made him sick to his stomach. He may not have marched Mercy towards the black door but it was his actions that had given her the orders.

He wished he could push through the invisible barrier and let himself drop to the ground. He knew that the weight of his guilt would carry him faster than gravity. He tapped his fingers as he counted off the deaths he was responsible for: his mother; more than likely his father; all of the contestants he had already beaten into the Death Room; Penny; and now Mercy too.

Suddenly, his room flashed with a deep green light. Luca dared not move.

Green blended into red.

Luca peered up to the camera, thinking that perhaps it was the source, but even before he turned fully he knew the light flooding the room was oozing down the walls. Luca shook his head to try to focus but all he could see was red, all the other details of the room faded from his sight. Everything was bathed in a blood red glow. The hairs began to rise on his arms and prickled at his neck. He could feel the tension spreading through his shoulders and bending his back in a curve. Before he knew it he had curled himself into a ball and was rocking back and forth with his back to the window.

Just as he felt his heart rate steadying another change occurred. The light began to alternate irregularly between blue and yellow, back and forth. Luca's ears buzzed and his head began to thump. Before he knew it, he could hear himself shouting for it to stop but his voice felt distant and detached. He gasped for breath and the air seared his throat.

Then everything went still. The lights faded and darkness crept back into the room. Silently, Luca watched as the gloom grew deeper. He slowly uncurled and peered behind him to the still city but even that began to blacken and the moonlight disappeared. The darkness grew more menacing, filling the air and seeping into Luca's skin. He began to scrub desperately at his arms and hands, pushing away from the perceived encroaching monster. He shuffled backwards until he could feel his spine pressed against the unyielding glass. There was nowhere to escape to. He wrapped his arms around his knees and tucked himself into a tiny space. There was nowhere to hide. Nowhere to hide from the darkness and nowhere to hide from his thoughts. He was consumed with fear.

Luca did not know how long he was trapped for. His arms ached and his fingers were stiff from holding himself together.

Abruptly, the room was transformed. Stark white light saturated the room. Luca clenched his eyes shut in pain. Even then he could see coloured dots and patterns swirling behind his eyelids. The intensity did not fade. Gradually, Luca opened his eyes and his vision adjusted but in this light he felt exposed, as if all his secret thoughts had been put on display. His face reddened in shame.

The room was bleached white under the glare but the window remained dark. The contrast caused a spark of warning to Luca. Crisp had said that Luca would be punished. With violence there is a small element he might have been able to control, Luca could attempt to defend himself and fight back.

Crisp had known that punishment was coming. Luca could not understand why he had responded to the torturous lights in such a way, but he did know that Tropolis were behind it. Why would coloured lights have such an effect on him? Colour had been so rare in Tropolis, so rare in fact, that there had only been one time that colour had been available. A shiver went through him when he thought of the boxes in the Connections Test. Luca could see that he had responded in a similar way during the test, but that should not affect him now. There must have been a trigger, something that would make him react this way. Luca swallowed as he realised that Tropolis had infected him. Tropolis had fixed that experience inside his mind and they had used a tiny tablet and injection to do so. What Tropolis had done had left Luca defenceless, how could you fight an unseen enemy?

Luca stretched out his arms, flexing his fingers and straightened his legs. He noticed the red blinking light of the camera. Someone had witnessed his ordeal; someone had managed to harm him without leaving an external mark.

Luca stumbled to the bed and climbed in pulling the covers over his head. He would not give Tropolis the pleasure of seeing any more tears.

Chapter 23

Click

Luca dared not move. They had evidently let him rest long enough.

He stared out into the darkness, knowing he did not have the strength for another round of torment from Tropolis.

He tensed as an unwelcome visitor was announced by the quiet rustle of the soft carpet as the door was pushed open.

He peered out from under the covers; the room was dimly illumined by moonlight through the large windows He saw movement and tall shadows by the door as someone crept towards him.

Luca instinctively checked the camera, but no red light blinked in the corner of the room. Lights out. He was not being watched, so no one would witness what was about to happen.

He panicked as he realised that he had nothing to hand to defend himself. Summoning the little energy he had left, he jumped out of bed and raised his fists. He would go down without at least some sort of fight..

'I'm not here to hurt you,' the male voice soothed.

The voice was familiar. The man walked slowly and steadily out of the shadows and into the cool moonlight.

Luca gasped. 'What are you doing here?' he asked. 'Have they sent you to finish me off?'

'Luca,' Crisp whispered. 'I need to get you out of here.'

'I'm not going anywhere with you,' Luca replied through gritted teeth, his mind racing. A traitor like Crisp offering to help him escape? It was bound to be another trick. He raised his fists higher, ready for a fight.

'I told you to be ready.'

Luca stepped back. 'What?'

'The message to be ready. We need to get going now, while the power is off.'

Luca blinked and shook his head. 'What are you talking about? You work for them. Why should I trust you?'

The door burst open. Someone darted across the room and charged into Crisp and they both landed heavily on the floor. Luca saw that Eban had pinned Crisp's arms back but there was little resistance from the Tropolite.

'What are you doing to him now?' Eban snarled. 'You won't get away with this.'

'I'm not doing anything,' Crisp protested, offering no resistance..

Eban glanced at Luca. 'They had locked the door,' he explained. 'I couldn't get back to you. Are you alright?'

Luca was lost for words. He slowly opened his fists and dropped his hands to his sides.

'What's he done?' Eban asked. 'Are you hurt?'

'I've not done anything. Get off me.'

Eban laughed and held him tighter.

Luca stepped forward .'I'm alright now but I don't think he has done anything.' He looked more closely at Crisp. 'In fact, he says he's the one who sent the message.'

Crisp turned his head slightly to face Luca. 'I did send the message,' he said earnestly. 'I'm here to get you out.'

'Out where?'

'Out of Tropolis,' Crisp replied.

'Why?' asked Eban.

'I have my reasons,' Crisp started, but Eban changed his grip. 'Alright! You aren't going to win the competition, they have realised that you cheated, and there are certain people who think you should be saved.'

'Who?' asked Luca.

'Friends of mine.'

'Why should we trust you?' Luca asked.

'Because without me you will both die,' Crisp stated with a hint of frustration. 'Tropolis will not keep you alive.' Eban looked up to Luca. 'And because I am an Outsider too,' Crisp said quietly.

'We don't have many more options,' Luca said to Eban.

Eban leaned on Crisp again. 'How are you going to get us out?' he questioned.

'There is a way that others have escaped.' Crisp tried again to address Luca and not Eban. 'Tropolis never discovered it.'

'How?' Luca pressed.

'You don't need to hold me so tight. I'm here to help you if you would let me,' Crisp hissed at Eban who had pushed his knee into his chest. 'Out with the waste and the rubbish,' Crisp grunted.

Luca placed his hand on Eban's shoulder. 'Let him go.' He turned to Crisp and offered his hand to help him to his feet. He could feel a tightening in his stomach.

Crisp stood and straightened his jacket. Without another word, even to Luca, Crisp led them from the bedroom.

They slowly followed him into the communal lounge, keeping close to the wall. Crisp had already crossed the room. Suddenly, a contestant's door opened just ahead of them. Luca shuffled back a step and grabbed Eban's arm as Thickset lumbered out, yawning. He quickly raised his fists.

'What the ...' Thickset began, startled. 'You thought you were going to get me, did you? I can take the two of you anytime!'

Crisp crept up behind Thickset. He swung his fist and punched him in the temple, following through as he twisted with the full force of his body. Thickset's expression went blank as his legs crumpled beneath him as he collapsed to the floor.

Everything was still and silent.

A sudden light came from Crisp's communicator.

'What are you doing?' Luca panicked.

Crisp frowned and whispered. 'Quietly now, follow me.'

He did not head for the lift, but crossed the lounge room. He stepped behind the food table that had the remnants of their meal still available, and ran his fingers down the corner of the wall. The edge began to twist towards them as a concealed floor-to-ceiling door opened up and Crisp went through.

Luca looked over at Eban, open mouthed. They rushed to follow.

The white landing was carpeted and the walls were covered in soft foam. Moonlight poured in through a large sky light allowed moonlight to pour in from above.

Crisp carefully and quietly closed the door behind them.

'This is a fire escape, not that we have ever had to use it.' Crisp's voice was muffled. 'Up here it is sound proofed, but further down you will need to be as quiet as you can. Understand?'

They both nodded.

Crisp was fast. He ran with ease down the stairs, and Eban followed him, taking two stairs at a time. Luca was exhausted from getting little sleep but the adrenalin was energising and encouraged him forward as he rushed after them both. He began to feel dizzy as he raced down flight after turning flight. He looked over the railing and could see the stairs twisting far below and fade into the darkness. His feet squeaked a little on the shiny floor as he sped round the bends. The gentle tapping of

Eban's steps in front and the possibility of escape carried him on into the unknown.

The roof light above was now a tiny square of dark blue. Crisp had slowed down. Luca puffed a little and wiped the sweat from his forehead with the hem of his shirt.

Crisp placed a finger to his lips and switched off the torch. Darkness engulfed them.

A long, thin slither of silver, vertical light appeared. Crisp's silhouette moved slowly into the open space beyond the door. Long shadows ran across the marble floor as the dim moonlight flooded through the glass ceiling. Eban and Luca copied Crisp's hushed movements. Each small noise echoed in the open space. But there was no one else to hear them.

They had stepped out into a familiar open space, but the night made it feel unsafe. Luca thought that they could head down the stairwell to the Maglev from here, but Crisp entered the doorway that led back into the holding area and past the shower rooms instead. The absence of people, even some security, made Luca nervous.

The sofas were still there, waiting for Thickset to sprawl on but there was no sign of any cables or recording equipment. Luca looked at the security cameras, again checking for any signs of being watched. The lights were out. This place seemed smaller somehow, without people busying themselves.

Crisp kept as close to the wall as possible. He beckoned them to follow.

Luca thought that they were heading for the dark and empty beautifying stations on the far side, but they stopped short.

Crisp pushed hard at the black door. A latch clicked and the Death Room door opened.

'I knew it!' Luca gasped, backing away. 'It's a trap!'

'No!' Crisp kept his voice low. 'Come on.' Luca did not move any closer to the door. 'This place is deserted, I arranged for there to be no guards. There is no one to stop us. This is the best way out. You need to trust me.'

'Why should I?' asked Luca.

Crisp stepped even closer and whispered, 'Because Willow would want you to.'

Chapter 24

'What do you know about my mother?' Luca said pushing Crisp through the door and up against the wall.

Eban hesitated, then followed them through the opening.

Crisp sighed and replied. 'She's my sister.' Luca stepped away. 'We don't have time for this. We need to hurry.'

'We do have time for this.' Luca would not be moved. 'That makes you my ...' Luca searched for the word, '... my uncle?'

'Yes.' Crisp smiled for the first time.

Luca closed his eyes for a moment as he realised he had family. He started to go through the times he had been in the company of Crisp and the conversations that they had. This shed fresh light on every one of them. But this man had betrayed Willow, his own sister, and left her Outside. He had condemned her whole family to living in poverty.

Luca scowled and was not certain he wanted a traitor as part of his family.

'So why were we on the Outside then?' Luca asked angrily poking Crisp in the chest.

'When I won the prize, I was told that my parents had died,' Crisp answered quietly, 'And that my sister could not be found.'

'You believed them?' Luca frowned.

Crisp nodded. 'At the time.'

Luca huffed and raised his hands.

'Gently mate,' Eban said patting Luca on the shoulder.

'I couldn't check,' Crisp began, trying to explain. 'At least, I couldn't check then.'

Luca shook his head. 'I presume you've checked since then though.'

'Yes, Luca, I have.' Crisp defended himself. 'Willow was killed in an accident at the docks, but Tropolis had known where she was up to that point. They lied to me. They didn't want her here. They could have honoured the deal of winning the Compassion Prize at any moment, but they didn't.' Crisp bowed his head. 'I told her I would bring her to Tropolis. I told her I would win and bring her here, to safety. They made a fool of me.'

Luca leaned against the opposite wall. 'You could've saved us.'

'I knew nothing about you. I never knew Willow had a child.' Crisp's voice quaked a little. 'It was only on that day at the gates that I had any idea you even existed.' He raised his hand and pointed at Luca's hair. 'Your mother had hair that exact shade of red, not at all common Outside, and there was something about your face that reminded me of her.' Crisp puffed out a light sigh. 'I looked you up on the databases as soon as I got back into Tropolis. I found that your mother, my sister, had been registered dead on the system but that number 57214 had been born a few years before her death. It was only by researching you that I found her too. All other details had been wiped or corroded. There wasn't even a record of your father. I didn't know for certain that it was you until too late. I couldn't stop you from entering the competition.'

Luca rubbed his face then looked over to Eban. He shrugged.

'I didn't want you hurt,' Crisp admitted, 'but there was little I could do. I am risking everything tonight. They worked out the stunt you pulled in the Intelligence Test and will be after you. I couldn't wait. I had to get you out. Get you to safety, for Willow's sake.'

Eban gave Crisp a hard stare and demanded, 'So get us out then.'

'Luca, do you still want me to help you?' Crisp asked. 'Can you forgive me?'

Luca nodded. 'I guess I understand why you never looked for us.'

Crisp smiled with relief. 'Thank you.'

A long, straight corridor stretched out to either side of them. To the right, the passage was dark but to the left warm squares of light could be seen in the distance. Luca moved towards the darkness, but Crisp lead them the other way.

'We'll be seen,' Eban warned.

'The machines charge during the day here. The power is still off for now. But if you don't hurry, we'll all be caught.' Crisp urged.

Luca checked for cameras. There were several dotted along the length of the corridor, but none appeared active.

Crisp walked briskly, and soon he was illuminated by the first window.

Luca peered in as he went past. It was just an empty white room.

They continued down the corridor. Window after window, empty room after room.

Crisp began to slow.

The next window framed a different scene. Machines obscured a clear view, but Luca could see two beds, separated by a glass wall. In each bed was a patient attached to a great number of wires and tubes. The person nearest to them, had one of the tubes connected to an arm, and at the other end, a silver machine. Dark red blood appeared to be filling the tube. A flat screen flashed with colours every few seconds. The tube exited from the far side of the machine. It was then threaded through a sealed rubber divider in the glass wall between the two beds and attached to the arm of the other person.

Crisp pushed the heavy door to the room open and quickly entered.

Luca and Eban followed.

Crisp had rushed over to the machine and was tapping buttons. Suddenly the screen went blank. He then moved away from the bed and began to tug on the tubes.

Luca was not paying attention. Suddenly, his focus was elsewhere. He stared in disbelief at the person laying silent and still in the bed.

Mercy was pale, but breathing.

Chapter 25

Luca clapped his hand to his mouth to stifle the shout. He dashed forwards and reached for her hand. It was warm but limp.

He turned to Crisp. 'Will she be alright?'

'Fine,' Crisp said looking up. 'The sedative needs to wear off.'

'What have they done to her?' asked Eban.

'I don't know,' Crisp answered. 'But nothing to harm her. She is too valuable to Tropolis to damage.'

'Valuable, how?' Luca wondered.

'Tropolis needs the Outsiders' blood and bodies. Tropolis is a dying city. The people here cannot survive without her or any of you.'

'They're killing us to give themselves life?' Luca questioned wrinkling his nose in disgust.

Crisp paused. 'Tropolis has been slowly decaying for years. They take what they need to survive.'

Mercy's fingers twitched.

'Mercy?' Luca whispered.

'Here. See if you can revive her.' Crisp poured water from a jug on the table onto a white towel and passed it to Eban who pressed it against Mercy's cheek. Crisp continued to pull wires and tubes away.

Suddenly there was a muffled voice from the other side of the glass. 'What do you think you are doing?' All three of them spun round in surprise. 'You can't just come in here and take her.'

The girl was sitting on her bed, still with the tube attached to her arm. She was not dressed in the same medical gown that Mercy had on, but wore the familiar white outfit that any of the contestants might wear. Her brown hair was a little wild from lying down. 'I need Mercy, you can't take her away from me.'

'We aren't taking anyone,' Crisp answered without further hesitation, standing up straight. 'That is, we need you to come with us to the next treatment room.'

'Really?' she asked, her hazel eyes squinting under the frown as she peered at Luca and Eban.

'Indeed,' Crisp continued. 'If you would kindly just step this way.'

She slid off the side of the bed. 'Will I need my shoes?' she asked innocently. Luca couldn't help noticing the way her hair framed her face in an extraordinary way that made her appear so vulnerable and fragile. Her face was somehow familiar.

Crisp nodded and turned to the boys. 'We can't leave her here,' he whispered. 'She has seen me and I'll get reported. You will have to take her with you. We don't have any choice.'

The girl opened the cabinet next to her bed, pulled out a small holdall and walked to the glass door. She looked behind her then slid it to one side.

'If you want Mercy to wake up, you'll need to take out that line. It's the one that gives the sedative.' The girl pointed to the final tube that was still attached. 'Let me help.' She approached the bed, dropped the bag to the floor and deftly removed the needle. She applied pressure to the site to stop the flow of blood and wrapped a long bandage in place at her elbow. 'Please, if you are going to take her, take me too. I know she isn't going for treatment.'

'Of course she is going for treatment.' Crisp stated.

'So why are Luca and Eban here then?' The girl gestured towards the boys. 'I've not missed any of the Network shows. I know that they are still in the Prize.'

Luca found it strange that she would know him at all.

'We need to leave Tropolis,' Luca said and Crisp tutted. 'They know that I cheated and will kill me.'

'Take me with you,' the girl said. Luca frowned as felt that she almost demanded it of Crisp.

'Why would you want to leave Tropolis?' Eban asked.

'I can't live here. Everything is wrong and I can't do anything about it. I am trapped. Please, take me.'

Eban and Luca exchanged glances. Crisp nodded his head.

'You won't be able to come back, no matter who tells you,' Crisp said. 'Do you understand?'

Luca thought that she glared at Crisp in response.

'I won't come back for anyone,' she promised and turned to Eban and Luca. 'You might want to grab a couple of extra blankets and bring that wheelchair over.' She bounced a little, excitedly, as she spoke. 'She won't be able to walk for a while.' The girl turned to Luca. 'Kelsee,' she held out her hand to Luca. 'My name is Kelsee.' He took it and she smiled. 'Thank you for agreeing to take me.' She turned to Eban and shook his hand too.

Luca grabbed the wheelchair and brought it closer to Mercy, laying a blanket over the seat. Crisp gently lifted Mercy from the bed, set her down in the chair and wrapped the blanket around her. Luca laid another blanket over her. Kelsee hung her bag from the handles.

'This way,' urged Crisp. 'Quietly!'

The corridor was still. The cameras were not activated, but Luca was anxious to get away from prying eyes. Crisp led them past the more windows. Luca peered in, a little nervous at what he might see. Room after room was set up much like Mercy's. The machines displayed coloured charts and results and the beds were occupied. As soon as he saw the pale complexion of Penny in the next room, Luca knew that the other beds would contain all the other contestants that had survived. The Death Room door did not lead to their death, at least not immediately, but was to stem the death of Tropolis.

The triumphant shouts of the Tropolites each time a contestant was taken to the door confused Luca now, more than ever. He wondered if Crisp was in a privileged position, knowing what happened in this place and if the rest of Tropolis knew the truth. He wasn't sure what he would prefer to believe. How could anyone be content with stealing life be it sudden or sucking it slowly and deliberately from Outside.

He rushed to catch up with Crisp. 'What about them?' he asked.

'No time. They are as bad as her.' Crisp pointed to Mercy asleep in the chair. 'You can't take any more.'

'We can't leave them,' Luca said.

'Yes, we can.'

Luca wanted to shout at his uncle, the Outsider turned Tropolite, who had promised to free them. But he could see that Crisp was right. He hesitated, frustrated at his powerless inability, and then followed after the man. He may not be able to release them now, but Luca was not going to forget about them. He would do something.

Crisp took them down a series of dark corridors, each looking so similar to the others that Luca was not sure he would ever find his way back. He stopped just short of some glass double doors and held his finger to his lips.

Two people walked past on the other side of the glass, chatting with one another. One held a torch in her hand while the other used a tablet of some kind that illuminated his face.

After waiting a few moments, Crisp gently pushed at the door. It clicked as he eased it open. He peered up and down the passageway and then beckoned for the others to follow.

The smell of disinfectant and cleaning fluids grew stronger as Crisp guided them towards a large door at a dead end. He leaned against it with all his weight. The heavy door slowly opened and a hissing sound of hydraulic pistons echoed through the silence. He pushed it just far enough to let the others through.

'The waste collection point is in deep under the building.' Crisp whispered as he switched on the light on his communicator and handed Eban a small, hand wound torch. 'This is the only access.'

'Not going to happen!' Kelsee pointed out. 'How are we going to get her down there?'

'The lift ...' Crisp slumped. 'No, the power is out.'

'Can't we carry her down the stairs?' Luca suggested.

'Too far and too narrow.' Crisp puffed. 'Not sure we could get her along the track either.'

Eban shook his head. 'We are not going to leave her here,' he said as he leaned over the wheelchair and checked Mercy.

'Is she awake?' Luca asked.

'No,' Kelsee whispered. 'She won't wake up properly for ages yet.'

Luca studied Mercy. She was warm and breathing deeply as if she were in a deep sleep.

'I have an idea,' Kelsee said. 'You may not like it though.' Luca looked up at her. 'I could take Mercy. We could go out the main doors. No one would stop me.'

'Well then, why don't we all do that?' Luca asked.

'Because everyone knows you,' Kelsee sighed. 'But I could wheel Mercy out. I just need to cover her face so that people don't know who she is.'

Luca tutted. 'That won't work!'

'It will work,' Crisp admitted being animated once again. 'If we bandage up her face, no one will question Kelsee.'

Luca and Eban both frowned.

'My peers are always having surgery,' Kelsee told them. 'It is part of being in Tropolis.'

'I don't know ...' Luca began.

'I will meet all of you at the dockside station. Please,' Kelsee begged, 'I don't want to be in Tropolis anymore. Luca, you need to trust me. I can get you away.' She looked longingly at him. 'Get *us* away from here.'

Luca was uneasy. He looked about, half expecting someone to discover them.

'What guarantee do we have that you are with us and won't get us caught?' Luca asked.

'I'm not sure I can prove it,' Kelsee said opening her hands to them. 'I know that you probably don't trust anyone in Tropolis right now, but you need to know that I'm not like them. I don't want to be like them.'

'If I may say something,' Crisp interjected. 'I think you can trust her. Kelsee has been quite vocal about what she believes to be Tropolis' problems over the last few months. She has not been very popular with the authorities.'

Kelsee smiled and nodded. 'My family are not very pleased with me.'

Her face was so open, and her eyes seemed to sparkle with pride, that Luca could feel himself wanting to trust her.

'Eban? What do you think?' Luca asked turning away from Kelsee's gaze.

'It may be the only way to do it. We can't go with mercy ourselves and I don't want to leave her here. I'm not sure there is another choice.'

'Alright,' Luca said and gently lifted Mercy's arm out from the blanket. He began to unwrap the bandage on her arm. 'I hope this will be long enough.' He handed the strip of cloth to Kelsee.

She beamed at Luca. 'That will work a treat.' She carefully wrapped it around Mercy's face, covering her nose. 'Not that there is anything wrong with her nose at all.' She took hold of Luca's hand and squeezed it. 'I won't let you down Luca, I promise.'

Luca caught his breath.

'Meet at the dockside station. On the right hand side where the cars are loaded into the barges,' Crisp clarified. 'It will take at least an hour to get there from this point. If there are any problems I would suggest that you meet at the Maglev service and cleansing point just past the station and into the tunnel.'

Kelsee nodded. 'I'll see you soon.' She leaned towards Luca and kissed him gently on the cheek. 'I'll get there as quickly as possible, try not to worry about her,' she said as she hugged Eban.

'Stay safe,' Luca insisted.

Crisp leaned on the door once again. It hissed as they opened and Kelsee walked confidently out into the main building with Mercy still asleep in the wheelchair.

Chapter 26

Luca ran his fingers through his hair as the door closed behind them.

Crisp was already out of sight and the faint glow from the light was disappearing down the narrow stairwell, so Luca followed after it.

The metal stairs clattered a little under their feet, but Crisp did not appear to be worried by the noise. The stairs spiralled down in a tight curve next to the lift shaft. Deeper and deeper the three of them travelled until Luca was certain that they were far underground.

The constant twisting made Luca's stomach churn. He was grateful when they eventually reached the last few steps. He looked up the central column and the stairs faded into the darkness.

Below the building, everything was grey and smelt of the heaps. The dull concrete was not polished and the surfaces did not gleam. Somehow, it was more human than above.

A large container sat beneath the closed lift doors. It was half full with rubbish sacks. Luca supposed that the rubbish was loaded at this point.

Crisp descended the final flight of concrete stairs so that the container towered over him. He continued along the tall, rectangular tunnel. Luca wiped the sweat from his forehead. It was warm in the tunnel and the large fans that were suspended from the ceiling were still.

'I can't take you much further,' Crisp called as he continued to walk. 'Lights out will be terminated soon and the power will back on. You need to get as far away from here before that happens.'

'You're not coming with us?' Luca asked.

'No,' Crisp replied, 'I am needed here.'

Luca looked at Crisp and narrowed his eyes suspiciously.

Crisp raised his open hands. 'If there are others that need to get out, I can help them. I have connections with the people already free.'

Luca sighed.

Crisp looked kindly at Luca. 'I can't leave Tropolis, at least, not yet. I can't go back to Outside.'

'I don't think we can either,' Luca said sadly. 'There is no way we will be able to glean and trade.'

Crisp nodded. 'You need to let the others find you, the ones that have escaped. They are out there and they aren't far away.' Crisp smiled a little. 'I don't know where exactly as it wouldn't be good for me to know those kinds of details. It would put them at risk if Tropolis found out I was working against it. But I do know that they are safe and I know they will be looking for you. They are aware of the escape plan for tonight. Tropolis is so sick that it doesn't have the man power to search for them anymore.'

'How is it sick?'

'People are reacting to everything.' Crisp explained, turning towards them. 'They cannot eat certain foods, they cannot come in contact with other things and even get out into the city. Kelsee is one of the more fortunate ones. Her family could afford the treatment. Others are not so wealthy and they are restricted to their homes and their close communities. No one is willing to help them as it is against the law. It is only by the likes of the Outsiders that are selected for the prize that any are helped at all.' Crisp continued along the tunnel. 'Tropolis won't come after you. It just can't.'

Luca frowned. 'Tropolis is really dying then.'

'It will continue to survive,' Crisp said. 'It continues to test Outsiders and is trying to replicate the antibodies that we have that fight against the severe allergies. They have been testing for years; for as long as I have been here at least. Things haven't got any worse, but they haven't got any better either. I don't think they are any nearer a cure.'

Mercy had been a vital part of that search for a cure, as were the other Outsiders. There was something that the contestants had that the Tropolites did not, including Kelsee.

'This treatment,' Luca asked, 'will it be enough for Kelsee?'

'It will keep her well for a while I guess,' Crisp said. 'What does it matter? As long as she gets Mercy to you.'

Luca balled his fists. This was the Crisp he recognised. 'She is helping us leave. I think you should show her a little more ... compassion.' Luca had never used the word as it seemed to mean different things to different people. But he knew what he meant.

Crisp turned again and raised his eyebrows, staring at Luca for a moment. 'There are some things you should know about that girl before you let yourself get carried away.'

'It doesn't matter what she has done,' Luca replied hotly. 'You should give her a chance.'

'So the fact that she is ... a Tropolite and is using you, and other Outsiders for medicine isn't a problem to you? She is one of the many that makes sure that the Compassion Prize continues. Doesn't that change your opinion?' Crisp spat. He waited, but Luca did not reply. 'Exactly!' Crisp turned his back on Luca and marched quickly ahead.

Luca stopped and closed his eyes.

'You alright?' asked Eban.

'It doesn't have to matter, does it?' Luca asked quietly looking at Eban.

'I don't know. Did she ask to get sick in the first place? We shouldn't judge her.'

Luca smiled sadly and shook his head. 'We don't need to be like him.'

'He's not so bad,' Eban replied. 'You need to remember what the Tropolites in power did to him and what they have made him do. They've damaged him and he is doing this little thing in defiance towards them.' Eban smiled at Luca. 'It is a small step, but a step in the right direction all the same. He is your uncle, your family. He hasn't finished his life's journey yet. Maybe, we need to show him a little of that compassion you were talking about.'

Luca and Eban jogged to catch up with Crisp.

The tunnel came to an abrupt end with a drop down to a maglev platform. A large machine was fixed firmly to the ground with bolts the size of Luca's waist. It had clamp like arms and a thick greasy barrel that turned. The machine could easily grip and tip the large waste container if it had been full.

Crisp pointed to the platform below. 'The rubbish removal Maglev trains run along this rail, through all the major buildings and on to the dock where the rubbish is loaded onto the barges.' Crisp led them down the ladder that was fixed to the ledge of the platform. 'You need to follow the rail all the way to the end of the line. It runs underground for the majority of the way. Nearer the docks you will be out in the open, so you will have to find cover when you get there. The power will be back on by then and no doubt they will be monitoring the cameras. Have you got that?'

'Follow rail, keep out of sight.' Eban laughed.

'Right,' Crisp sighed. 'I wish you the best Luca.'

'I'll not forget what you have done for us.' Luca held out his hand.

Crisp reached for it and grasped it. He pulled Luca close and hugged him. 'I'm so sorry that I wasn't there when your mum died, and I'm sorry I couldn't look after you.'

'That is not your fault,' Luca said pulling away so that he could see Crisp's face. Luca was glad that he really meant it. 'But promise me something.' Crisp looked at his nephew. 'Please, you've got to get out of this place.' Luca could see the damage this place had done to his uncle. 'You need to have freedom too.'

'One day, Luca, I will, I promise.'

'If you don't, I'll come and get you myself.'

Crisp laughed. Luca liked the sound of it. He leaned forward and hugged him once more then walked away, not turning back. He listened to the sound of Crisp's footsteps over the metal rungs of the ladder behind him and then there was nothing but his own and Eban's shuffling noises.

The beam of light from the small torch was narrow but bright. Eban lit the edge of the platform and Luca lowered himself down. The metal rail, for the Maglev, was knee height off the concrete base and continued endlessly into the darkness.

Eban shone the beam up onto the ceiling and out into the tunnel. There were no decorative features or landmarks. This platform was not for any purpose but to remove waste, unlike the intimidating entrance into Tropolis.

Eban hummed to himself and Luca was grateful for his relaxed friend. 'Let's go then,' he said.

It was difficult to measure the passing of time. The tunnel was featureless and dark. Luca thought that perhaps the tunnel just went in a circuit, since the next few rubbish loading platforms were identical to the one they had entered at.

'The numbers are different though,' Eban had pointed out when Luca finally questioned the path they were taking. 'Up on the walls by the platforms.' Eban was correct. They were moving forward but Luca's sense of panic was still near the surface.

The darkness of the tunnel left Luca disorientated. The smell of disinfectant mingled in the still air with the lingering tang of rubbish. There was nothing to hear except his own breathing and footsteps on the concrete, even Eban did not hum. The tension was tightening around him and he could feel his body responding as his shoulders stiffened. He needed a distraction.

He straightened his shirt as he wondered about Mercy and Kelsee. But that did not ease the pressure. He could not help but worry about them. He wanted to explain to Mercy, to apologise for the mistake he had made. He wanted to show her he was grateful that she had chosen to take his place. He hoped that he would have the chance. He wished that Kelsee would keep Mercy safe. And even in the short time that he had with Kelsee, he wanted her to be secure too.

Eventually, a spot of light could be seen in the darkness, it slowly grew larger the more they walked. Even the air seemed to move and drift. Luca was certain that they would soon be by the dock and that Mercy and Kelsee would be waiting for them. The thought loosened the knot in his stomach.

The soft dawn light filtered into the tunnel through the greenery outside. Luca increased his pace. He could feel the oppressive weight of the darkness lifting and wanted to be in the fresh air once more. The leaves framed the tunnel and formed thick walls of vegetation either side of the track the same shape as a Maglev train. He emerged from the closeness and echoes formed by the tunnel to the loud chattering and tuneful chorus of unseen birds. The sound was intense. Luca had never heard anything like it before. Their joy and freedom lifted his heavy heart and infused it with hope.

The green path stretched out before them. Luca breathed deeply, half expecting a rancid stink of death, but instead a rich earthy smell filled his senses. Luca shook his head and sighed.

'What is it?' Eban asked.

'Tropolis has damaged me,' Luca began, turning to Eban. 'I can't trust my reactions to colour anymore.' Luca noticed his hands were shaking a little and stuffed them into his pockets. 'They've ruined how I see colour. See this?' Luca looked around at the vegetation. Eban nodded and smiled. 'Exactly, I should be happy to see it, I can see and hear the life here, but inside I'm having to fight the feeling of death and decay. They've imprinted the emotions and sensations from the connections test into my mind.'

'Well, I guess you need to imprint what it really is then.'

Luca snorted. 'Not that easy. They used chemicals to get it into my mind.'

'You know what, the body is an amazing thing; it can repair itself. You should start seeing yourself differently. You aren't a Tropolite. You don't need to think and act the way they do.'

'I'm not that sure who I am right now,' Luca admitted and turned away.

'You're Luca,' Eban said patting Luca's shoulder. 'You were the one that figured the way out; the one that trusted in others when all around you there was hatred and rivalry; the one that has come to life. That is all you need to know. It doesn't have to be complicated.'

They carried on, not speaking anymore, but Luca knew that Eban had been right. He just wished it could be that simple.

Soon, concrete buildings began to line the track and the greenery faded away. Windowless walls of large industrial buildings directed Luca and Eban towards the docks.

Luca peered about, expecting to see someone watching, but this area seemed deserted. The gaps between the buildings gave small glimpses into a less-polished area Tropolis. There were no glass encrusted skyscrapers or minimal white facades.

The whirring of a machine on the other side of the wall began suddenly, the gentle hum from the Maglev track and a dirt encrusted carriage wheeled slowly past the gap between the buildings. Luca and Eban pulled themselves tight against the concrete wall. Luca dared to look into the carriage, there was no person inside only a screen with numerous flickering lights. The motor seemed to tick as it turned the corner following the line painted onto the road. The power was back on. Tropolis was awake.

'They'll know we've gone,' Eban whispered. 'Come on.'

The first glimpse of the sea glistening and sparkling in the early morning sunlight made something in Luca's soul jump. He was instinctively being pulled towards it, freedom was nearly in his grasp. Seagulls called familiarly to one another as they swooped on the salty breeze overhead. Luca and Eban kept to the shadow of the buildings as they continued along the rail.

A faint rumble came from behind them. Luca turned. The single headlight signalled the Maglev train was speeding towards them.

'Run!' he yelled.

Chapter 27

Luca and Eban sprinted. The buildings either side stretched out before them with no breaks. Still the train came mindlessly closer.

Luca was falling behind Eban, his exhausted body was not responding. He peered back and panicked, forcing a little more speed out of his weary muscles.

Eban turned, slowed then reached back, grabbed Luca and pulled him forward. Luca stumbled, but managed to keep up.

They rushed to the end of the wall and just skimmed the corner when the Maglev sped past with its half dozen cars.

Luca panted and doubled over while Eban lay flat out on the concrete.

Once he had recovered a little by taking calming breaths, Luca peered around the corner.

The train had continued down the track for a short distance but it had stopped just past a bend in the track. The last car could be seen.

'We're nearly there,' Luca said and offered his hand to Eban. 'You ready?'

Eban nodded, got to his feet and followed Luca.

The noise of the falling rubbish into an echoing metal container somewhere below filled the air but was evidently not disturbing anyone. The buildings remained still and the roads were silent. The area was not for housing Tropolites, but full of factories and industrial units. No one would choose to live among the workings of Tropolis when the city was clean and carefully planned. Everything here seemed to be automated or operated remotely.

Luca and Eban approached the Maglev train. The sea breeze was keener here and swept the familiar smell of rubbish towards them. The front cars had been tipped and the contents emptied, crashing into a barge below. They had made it to the dock.

As he approached, Luca's heart raced. He was not expecting the massive drop beside the train onto the barge that was moored at the dockside. To the left of the train there was a raised platform, but to the right the floor was cut away so that the rubbish could fall. There was no barrier to stop people from falling. He moved closer and saw the rubbish flooding the barge from the series of cars further up the train.

They had made it to the dock.

Eban pulled Luca to a crouch behind the last car. Luca's foot slipped a little and he gasped.

'Camera,' Eban warned, 'up on the platform.'

Luca glanced up. 'Any others?'

A loud clicking began and the cars began to tilt once again to their upright position.

'We've got to get out of here.' But even before Luca could finish, the train moved. Luca flinched. It began to move further up the track.

'Just follow it,' Eban said.

Luca stooped and tried to keep up with the train as it moved on. The cut away section next to the rail was narrow, almost as if the rail was suspended in the air. The concrete that the rail was fixed to was just the breadth of Luca's feet. He wished he could cross over the rail to the other side but the camera would be sure to see him. As it was, he feared they would be caught on camera, so he hoped that if they stayed close to the train their movement would not be noticed.

The Maglev stopped again and the last three cars began to tilt. Rubbish poured from the containers in a mass of crunching and ripping sounds. The smell of rotting food and waste wafted up. Luca gagged.

The onslaught died down and the last few items slipped from the tilted cars and floated to the barge deck below. The mechanism under the cars began to click and they righted themselves once again.

From the ridge Luca had a bird's eye view of the barge below, full of rubbish. A thick wire mesh was automatically sliding high over the mound, enclosing the load.

Eban tapped Luca on the shoulder and pointed to the bars that ran up the side of the container. They had notches in them and would have held the container in its sideways position. 'Grab onto the container,' Eban said.

Luca leaned over the edge and reached for the bar. He pulled himself onto the container wall. He quickly moved over and made room for Eban. The bar was far enough away from the car's wall for him to slide his foot into place between the teeth and take his weight. The Maglev began to move.

The carriages were not taken far.

Within a few moments, the Maglev was stationary again in a tall damp tunnel.

Luca perched on the side of the container that now appeared to be floating in mid-air. There was no floor below, only darkness. Luca's fingers ached and he was starting to panic.

'Luca!' a female called from the other side of the container. 'Luca! You've got to get out of here,' she was urgent. 'Quick!'

Luca clung to the container.

'It's me, Kelsee,' she shouted. 'Please you've got to move.'

Luca began to clamber up the side. At the top of the container, the bar stopped. He grasped the slime-covered opening and pulled himself to the container roof edge. Crawling to the other side, he spotted Kelsee stood on the slender kerb at the side of the tunnel wall.

'You are going to have to jump.'

'There's not enough space,' Luca said. He turned to Eban who now crouched behind him. 'What do you think?'

'Is there nothing to hold?' Eban asked.

Luca shook his head and shifted over a fraction to let Eban move forward.

Eban carefully leaned over the side. 'Maybe, we use the curve of the container and push off the side.'

Luca pointed to the gap between the container and the kerb where Kelsee was fidgeting.

'We could wait until it moves,' Luca suggested.

'No time!' Kelsee yelled. 'The boiling water will come on any moment. Jump, please.'

A hiss came from above.

Eban slid fast down the side and pushed off the side. He landed on his feet and Kelsee pulled to steady him. He made it look simple.

'Just do it, Luca,' Eban shouted. 'We'll catch you.'

Luca swallowed hard. He crouched at the top of the container, took a deep breath, then let his body slide down the smooth metal. He slammed his feet against the side and kicked off with his arms outstretched. Eban grabbed his hand and his elbow, while Kelsee gripped hold of his other hand. His toes caught the concrete strip as he landed. He stepped forward quickly.

'Move!' Kelsee shouted and pushed them to the far end of the tunnel where the front of the Maglev was waiting.

The hissing grew and suddenly jets of water from above shot out causing the container to tremble and rumble. Clouds of steam poured over the sides. Then the hissing began high up on the wall.

'Get under the gate.' Kelsee pointed to where the Maglev had stopped just short of two vast wooden doors. She jumped from the kerb at the side, onto the plinth supporting the end of the rail rested on and rolled under the gap at the bottom of the timber doors. The boys followed, as strong jets of boiling water began to spray against the outside of the container.

Steam billowed out under the gates. Kelsee led them out into the middle of the road that had been built between the station and a line of buildings with large metal shutters. She looked up into the sky and sighed.

Eban asked, 'Where's Mercy?'

'Safe, don't worry.' Kelsee turned to Luca and hugged him. 'I thought you were gone for good.'

'How did you know we were there?' Luca asked pulling back from her a little. He noticed how the sunlight caught her hair with streaks of auburn.

'I saw you follow the train then disappear. You looked like you were hiding, then I saw the camera and understood what you were doing. I hoped that you had climbed on somehow. The cleansing tunnels are not designed for people. It's all automated.' Kelsee grinned. Her teeth were perfectly straight, but it was the colour in her cheeks that caught Luca's attention. Was she blushing? 'I'm so glad you got out of there,' she said as the sound of water gushing into a pool and a large plume of steam rose into the air. 'I don't know what I would have done if you got scolded.'

'Glad you were there,' Luca said quietly. 'Thanks for catching me.'

Kelsee laughed. 'Anytime!'

'Er guys,' Eban said. 'I think we have a slight problem.' He pointed as the barge laden with rubbish pulled away from the dockside. 'I think our ride has left without us.'

Kelsee smiled. 'I have had a better plan. Follow me.'

Chapter 28

A long, narrow alley ran between the buildings. Luca looked back and could see the steam lazily drifting from under the wooden gate. Kelsee called to him and he followed her and Eban into the shadows.

Luca shivered. His feet scuffed on the gritty floor, making an intense sound. Kelsee put her finger to her lips. He tried to be silent.

Kelsee cautiously peered into the space beyond the passage. The gentle clinking of metal, like a series of tuneful bells, irregularly pierced the air. She straightened up and walked out into the morning sun. She beckoned the others to follow.

The pristine paved walkway stretched out and faced the front side of the shops. The railings on the other side provided a viewing ledge for the marina below. The window displays were minimal and stylish, full of mirrors and lights, draped clothing and furnishings, glittering jewels and flashes of colour. Everything oozed extravagance, yet there were no price tags.

Kelsee walked briskly ahead. Luca was fascinated by all the trinkets and began to slow. He stared at the textured oil painting of the sea scene propped up in an artist's easel. There were beautiful things in Tropolis if you looked hard enough.

He felt the tug at his arm.

'These shops do just fine without you,' Kelsee said sadly. 'The wealthy keep them in business.'

Movement caught his attention. A tall man was walking towards them dressed in Tropolite white with a dark belt and hat.

'Act normal,' Kelsee hissed.

'Morning miss. You are out early' he said.

'Errand for my grandfather.' Kelsee smiled and hurried on.

He passed her with a quick smile and nodded to Luca and Eban.

She turned to a small gate at the end of the paving and swiped a silver card over the scanner. The machine beeped and the gate slowly slid open.

Luca peered at the silver card. He rubbed his thumb over his wrist. It was the little things that Tropolis had done to Outside that had made them him, somehow, less human.

The galvanised path gradually sloped down to the wooden quay where all the yachts were moored, still shaded from the early morning sun in the marina basin, and rocking gently in the breeze. Kelsee increased her speed.

Their feet pattered on the metal and then tapped on the wooden boards. Kelsee ignored the tall masted boats and was virtually running towards the largest yachts. She reached the boat docked in the middle and clambered up the short ladder and onto the deck then disappeared out of sight. Luca could hear a familiar female voice and climbed quickly after her.

'Mercy!' He dashed through the doorway and flung his arms around her. He was overwhelmed with gratitude to see her no longer resembling a patient but on her feet and dressed in normal Tropolite clothes. 'I'm so sorry for what I did,' he whispered in her ear, 'and I'm so glad you are safe.'

Eban ran in and hugged them both. Soon all three of them were laughing and jumping together. Kelsee giggled quietly from the side. Luca leaned over and welcomed her into their huddle. At last he felt he could breathe deeply again.

Luca glanced out the door and saw several people rushing alongside the shop fronts on the pavement above. He stopped jumping.

'They've found us,' Luca pointed to the commotion.

'Mercy, can you drive this?' Kelsee asked quickly dragging her to the wheel and punching in a code. The engine started with a slight tremble and then constant hum. She didn't wait for her to answer. 'Pull this lever to go backwards when I tell you, then push it forwards, but not too fast afterwards. You two come with me.' She climbed down the ladder and Luca followed.

'Eban stay there and catch the ropes. We might need you to help.'

Luca saw the Tropolite security bunched up at the gate on the far side.

Kelsee was hurriedly untwisting the rope that attached the bow to the dockside. She gathered it up in her hands and tossed it to Eban.

Luca began to untie the rope at the stern.

'Luca, wait!' Kelsee cried. 'Mercy, do it now!'

The boat began to move backwards. The fenders squeaked a little and bulged as the boat pushed against the dockside. The bow slowly twisted out from the decking where it had been moored and from behind the boat in front. It continued to twist until it faced the open canal between the other moored boats.

'Untie it now, but keep it wrapped round just once and then climb up,' Kelsee instructed not looking at him.

'I'll throw the rope to Eban. Let me help you.' Luca said tossing the messy coil of rope. Kelsee fidgeted and looked towards the approaching security guards. 'You can't stay here,' Luca said suddenly gauging Kelsee. 'Climb up first.'

She shook her head. 'I've thought about it. I'll be no use to you,' Kelsee said quietly.

'Please. I want you to,' Luca said calmly despite the sound of many feet on the metal path. 'What is here for you?'

Kelsee paused for a moment and looked Luca. 'Nothing.'

Luca pushed her towards the ladder and she clambered up. He climbed after.

'Forward now!' Kelsee yelled to Mercy, waiting by the throttle and wheel.

A sudden thrust forward sprayed water over the wooden decking and made Luca slip down a step. Kelsee reached out and grabbed him. Eban dropped the rope and pulled them both to the safety of the deck.

The end of the rope uncoiled from the mooring bollard and slipped into the water just as the men pounded to the dockside, out of breath and red faced.

'You have got to come back,' the man, who had been so polite before, shouted. 'Stop!' He ran up the wooden decking, following them as far as he could. Mercy guided the boat to the bend in the canal and the view of open water filled Luca with hope

'Please,' the guard yelled at the top of his voice. 'You must come back, Miss Barret!'

Chapter 29

'Barret?' Luca turned to Kelsee. 'As in Harland Barret?'

'My grandfather.' Kelsee sighed and hung her head. 'Take the boat. I'll let you,' she said sadly. 'I'll just make sure the tracker is turned off first.' She reached over to the dashboard and flicked a switch. She bit down on her lip and walked out of the cabin doorway.

'Wait!' Mercy turned. 'Where are you going?' she asked.

'I can swim back to the marina from here,' Kelsee said lifting up the seat and pulling out a lifejacket. She refused to look any of them in the face.

Luca grabbed her arm. 'Why would you do that?' She looked down at his hand on her arm and she sighed, smiling sadly. He loosened his grip. 'I thought you wanted to come with us.' He could feel his heart beating hard in his chest. 'You said there was nothing for you in Tropolis.'

'I have stuff in Tropolis, you know, money and I guess, my family, not that I'm like any of them.'

'So why go?' Luca asked.

'I'm a Barret.'

Luca frowned. 'And?'

211

'And that makes me the worst type of Tropolite.'

Eban crossed his arms. 'Since when does a name mean anything?'

'This name means everything here,' Kelsee said. 'It means power and influence. It also means suffering and greed. I am the granddaughter of Harland Barrett, the so called founder of Tropolis and instigator of the Compassion Prize. I don't think you will want me with you now.'

'You believe that?' Luca said angrily. Kelsee shrugged her shoulders. 'You don't need to be defined by a name or your family. Those things are determined by your birth. Your grandfather may have built Tropolis, and his identity has been revealed by his actions, but you are not building to his design. You are a fresh design, a different person. You cannot be truly defined by someone else's history. It is only you that can determine who you become.'

Mercy increased the boat's speed. 'When we first came to Tropolis,' she said calmly and turned, 'we had no known names. We were just numbers. But we got to choose what to be called. The same goes for you.'

'I don't want to be a Barret.'

'Then don't be,' laughed Eban. 'You have the choice. You don't have to live with someone else's identity.'

'You mean that?' Kelsee questioned. 'Really? Even though I am putting you in danger just by being here?' She raised her eyebrows evidently worried. 'The danger is real. My grandfather will not want this being known.'

'You made this escape possible.' Mercy's eyes were moist with tears. 'I thought you were doing all this so that we could be together,' she said.

Kelsee darted forward to Mercy and hugged her tightly. 'Thank you!' she whispered as tears flowed down her cheeks. Eban took the wheel as Mercy comforted Kelsee.

Luca wrapped his arms about himself. He had not realised that his identity had changed since being in Tropolis. He had no home yet had never felt more comfortable with himself. He had been accepted and welcomed by Mercy and Eban, just as Kelsee would now experience. His survival was not based on an act such as gleaning and a need to exist. It was now an attitude and sense of being an individual. He saw himself as a human who had weaknesses yet was now capable of actually living. The taste of freedom intoxicated him. He couldn't help but giggle to himself.

A beep sounded from the dashboard and they all fell silent.

'Kelsee honey,' the male voice called from the communicator, 'I need you to turn round and head back home. You've had your fun but enough is enough.' He paused and then his voice became angry. 'This is not amusing. You are making me out to be a fool and I will not stand for it. You have one hour to return my boat and those Outsider vermin or I will personally set the guard on you.'

Kelsee puffed. 'My loving grandfather,' she introduced with a gesture to the speaker. 'As self-centred as ever.' She turned to Eban. 'What do you want to do? We probably will have that time, he won't want this news spreading so he will come after me.'

Eban shifted the boat into full speed away from the marina and began to hum. 'I don't know where to go.' He gazed out of the cockpit window. 'But I guess if we follow that rubbish barge, we will get somewhere.'

Luca looked on his friends with affection. They would welcome Kelsee into their fold without prejudice and accept her for who she was. She was related so closely to the man who had outlawed charity and created the prison of Outside. This knowledge should have made him detest her. But he saw through all those potential labels and knew that there was a connection between them.

The boat jolted over the slight waves. The barge had set a course out to sea but in line with the shore.

Tall white pillars had been carved out of the cliff by the consistent sea. They stood like an entry gate.

The barge rounded the furthest pillar and disappeared. Eban guided the boat after it.

The land mass began to dip and the stony ground became almost level to the beach. It jutted out, wide but low, exposed to the elements and deserted save for the one overwhelming feature. An unnatural line of concrete interrupted the horizon and blocked the view. But Luca knew what lay beyond.

The wall was high and stretched the entire width of the land. It waded deep into the sea and was wide enough to isolate anyone on the other side. They would not be able to consider the possibilities beyond it.

He was looking at the wall to Outside.

The hair on his arms prickled as he stared at the thing that had held so much power over him. From this side, set at the pinnacle of the vast landscape, it appeared small and meaningless. It could not hold back the ocean and it sliced such a small area of land. Luca's perspective was changing. From this side the wall was merely holding the people from Outside back. It controlled them by focussing them on the smaller picture. From this side, Luca could possibly gain freedom and not just dream of it. What would happen if Outsiders were free?

Mercy stood silently next to him.

Kelsee asked quietly. 'What is this place?' Luca smiled sadly and Kelsee shook her head in disbelief. 'Home?' Luca nodded. 'I'm so sorry. I had no idea.'

A voice sounded out over the water, amplified and bouncing off the waves.

'This is a message from Campion Headquarters, do you read me?' the female asked.

Luca looked all around them, but could not see here anywhere that could be the source of the message. 'Campion,' he said. 'That's the flower – you know, the one on the book and the tattoo.' He waved his arms. 'We read you Campion,' he yelled.

'Reduce knots and prepare to be boarded from the port side. We are coming to get you.'

'Who are they?' Kelsee whispered.

'I think they are the free people.' Luca said excitedly. 'They've found us!'

'This is what you want?' Kelsee asked.

Luca nodded. 'Totally.'

She pointed to the left side of the boat. 'They'll be coming from that side. And they want you to slow down, Eban.'

The sea appeared dark and empty. There seemed to be no other vessels.

The boat swayed more noticeably now that it was no longer following the barge. The waves lapped against the hull.

'There!' Mercy shouted and pointed but Luca could not make out anything.

Luca blinked at the water, there was something moving but it could easily have been just a trick of the light. Suddenly he realised that a small boat was pulling up alongside them. It had a roof that shimmered and undulated, moving in a way that almost perfectly camouflaged it when at a distance; but now it was close up, the edges of the roof gave it away. But it had been incredibly effective.

Luca caught the wet rope that someone threw as a hand pushed and folded the roof back. A tanned man sat at the engine rudder and a slight woman looked up at the large yacht. Neither of them wore white.

'Luca, Mercy,' she said nodding in greeting. 'But you are not Eban, you're a Barret...'

'... this is Kelsee,' Eban interrupted, resting his hand on her shoulder as he stepped out of the cockpit. 'She is with us.'

'We are not authorised to take her.'

Luca stepped in front of Kelsee and glared at the woman.

'But we are,' Eban said and turned to Luca and Mercy.

'Absolutely,' Luca replied. He could hear the drumming of his heart. 'If she stays, I stay.'

'We all stay,' Mercy agreed.

The woman frowned. 'Very well. I suppose she might be of some use. On your head be it.' She grabbed a sack from behind her, and climbed on board. 'All of you – gather your things and get in our boat. I'll only be a few moments.'

Kelsee dashed below deck and appeared a little while later with a bulging white satchel. Luca remembered his own bag, containing the items that meant something to him. He did not begrudge her for wanting to take something with her.

The slight woman was fiddling with the wires underneath the dashboard. She then straightened up.

'Miss Barret,' she said, indicating Kelsee. 'Do you know how to set the auto pilot?' Kelsee nodded. 'We need full speed, whatever that is on this monster, and head it back to the marina. Oh, and this vessel needs to be tracked by Tropolis. I noticed you disengaged the tracking system. Please turn it back on.'

Kelsee flicked the switch, tapped the screen and entered a code. 'Done.' The boat began to move dragging the smaller boat in its wake.

Luca took Kelsee's bag and then helped her into the smaller craft. Within minutes they were all on board the smaller, camouflaged boat.

The looped rope was released and the large yacht turned in a wide arc and headed back to the marina leaving the little boat drifting and floating alone on the sea.

'Welcome aboard!' the man said in a husky voice as the woman unfolded the roof above them. 'Let's get back to headquarters.'

The engine spluttered into life and the small boat turned towards the last white pillar of the cliff.

Luca sat next to Kelsee while Mercy and Eban were on the bench opposite. The Campion crew were busy steering and working the radio.

Suddenly there was a loud boom and a flash of orange light flared.

Kelsee covered her mouth with her hand; Mercy ducked; Eban spun round quickly; Luca watched with eyes wide open.

Luca saw the yacht encased in a massive fire ball.

'Well,' the man at the rudder said laughing, 'They won't think you survived that!'

Kelsee shuddered and a quiet sobbed emerged. Luca put his arm around her. He knew what it was like to say goodbye to everything you knew and then face the unknown. He had never had to face that by himself. She leaned into him and hid her face in his jumper. He sighed. Luca held her close. 'You will be alright. You are in the best place.'

Mercy shuffled to Kelsee's other side and held her hand. 'Luca knows how to be a good friend.'

'I have some amazing friends that would do anything for me,' Luca said smiling at Mercy and Eban. 'They have taught me everything I know. Hopefully I have picked up a few good habits.'

'Well, I've never really had friends before,' Kelsee admitted. 'People would use me but not really care about me.'

Luca smiled and gripped Kelsee's shoulder. 'You are part of us now. You'll soon know what true friendship is.'

They all watched the fuel-fed flames and black smoke. Luca turned towards the wall as it disappeared over the horizon. He hoped that his father and the other Outsiders were witnessing the signal as it rose high into the air.

Other books by Katy Hollway ...

The Times of Kerim

Bruja hunts her, hungry for power. Japh waits for her, trusting in a promise. The Remnant plans for her. And I guide, watching as the storm begins.

Kerim is tired of running. She has escaped. Her wounded hands ache and her weary body needs rest. She hides in the shadow of a strangely familiar rock crevice. Japh has been waiting years to find her, but is he prepared for the perilous events that will unfold at her discovery?

Is she ready to listen to me, her messenger? Is she ready to step into her destiny?

Kerim discovers that mankind is not all the same. That some are called to be saved.

The Days of Eliora

Si dominates her, eager for respect Caleb notices her, detecting someone unique The Remnant shuns her And I watch over, as turmoil encompasses the land Eliora lives between worlds. Disowned by one and mistrusted by the other; she has no identity. Finding solace in conflicting friendships will shape her future beyond recognition. Caleb brings relief to her testing days, but can he bring startling revelation about who she really belongs to. Will she still her confusion and listen to my message? Is her heart prepared for the battle?

Eliora does not fit. Neither the palace nor the settlement offers her a place to be who she is called to be. Join Eliora as she discovers her calling amid the slavery of her people and the tyrannical Pharaoh. Discover the unfolding story through both the human and supernatural realm.

Lightning Source UK Ltd.
Milton Keynes UK
UKOW05f2142070317
296055UK00011B/110/P